Do you like romantic comedies?

Then you'll love Harlequin Romance's new
miniseries—where love and laughter are guaranteed!

*The Fun
Factor*

Warm and witty stories of falling in love

**Look out for the next
in The Fun Factor series…coming soon.**

Dear Reader,

This was such a fun book to write! I'd had Harlan's character in my mind for years, and had been waiting to find the right story to fit him—and the right woman to challenge him. Harlan Jones is my idea of a cowboy—sexy, strong, yet with a soft side to him that takes Sophie by surprise. I hope you enjoy reading Harlan and Sophie's story as much as I enjoyed writing it!

I love the coffee-shop setting, too. I spend a lot of my time sitting in coffee shops while I write. The baristas are fabulous—they remember how I like my lattes, which flavor of tea is my favorite and that I like all the fixings on my oatmeal in the morning. When I created Sophie's coffee shop, I tried to create the kind of environment I like to frequent. There's a whole cast of characters in Sophie's shop—pretty much like the interesting cast of characters I find in my local coffee shop.

I love to hear from readers, so please write to me at P.O. Box 5126, Fort Wayne, IN, visit my website at www.shirleyjump.com or read my recipes and life adventures at my blog, www.shirleyjump.blogspot.com. Tell me about your favorite coffee shop, or share your favorite latte flavor!

Shirley

SHIRLEY JUMP

How to Lasso a Cowboy

The Fun Factor

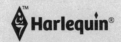

™ **Harlequin**®

TORONTO NEW YORK LONDON
AMSTERDAM PARIS SYDNEY HAMBURG
STOCKHOLM ATHENS TOKYO MILAN MADRID
PRAGUE WARSAW BUDAPEST AUCKLAND

Recycling programs
for this product may
not exist in your area.

ISBN-13: 978-0-373-17723-3

HOW TO LASSO A COWBOY

First North American Publication 2011

Copyright © 2011 by Shirley Kawa-Jump, LLC

New York Times bestselling author **Shirley Jump** didn't have the willpower to diet, nor the talent to master under-eye concealer, so she bowed out of a career in television and opted instead for a career where she could be paid to eat at her desk—writing. At first, seeking revenge on her children for their grocery-store tantrums, she sold embarrassing essays about them to anthologies. However, it wasn't enough to feed her growing addiction to writing funny. So she turned to the world of romance novels, where messes are (usually) cleaned up before The End. In the worlds Shirley gets to create and control, the children listen to their parents, the husbands always remember holidays and the housework is magically done by elves. Though she's thrilled to see her books in stores around the world, Shirley mostly writes because it gives her an excuse to avoid cleaning the toilets and helps feed her shoe habit. To learn more, visit her website at www.shirleyjump.com.

Praise for Shirley Jump

"Shirley Jump winds up A Bride for All Seasons with *Marry-Me Christmas,* a sweet story with terrific characters and a well-constructed plot."
—*RT Book Reviews,* four stars

About *New York Times* bestselling anthology *Sugar and Spice:*
"Jump's office romance gives the collection a kick, with fiery writing."
—*PublishersWeekly.com*

To my little brother, Fred. Remember,
I'm never going to be too old to pick on you.
I love you!

CHAPTER ONE

HARLAN JONES set the sixth chair of the month on his front stoop, removed his cowboy hat and brushed the sweat off his brow before replacing the headgear. If he kept up like this, he'd either have to get married and have twenty kids or start giving the damned things away. Or, better yet, quit building them. If he was a smart man, he'd put the circular saw and drill away for good. Get over this stupid fantasy that he could be a woodworker.

A soft barrel-shaped body brushed against his leg. Harlan chuckled, leaned down and scratched Mortise behind the ears. The golden retriever's tail slapped happily against his rump, and he snuggled closer. Tenon, not to be left out, brought her slender golden body into the mix, and slobbered onto Harlan's hand.

"A sane man wouldn't waste time building chairs he isn't going to sell," Harlan said to the dogs. Because they never argued back.

"A sane man focuses on a job with benefits." Harlan moved away from the dogs, heading into the garage he'd converted into a woodshop, and started to put his tools away. "One that has a nice retirement package."

Mortise dropped to his haunches in the doorway and panted. Tenon bounded off after a squirrel in the yard.

Harlan exited the garage, then shut the door. Was it

crazy to be talking to his dogs? Probably, but hell, it was only him and the mutts here. Had been for six weeks, ever since he'd moved from Dallas to this tiny rental house in Edgerton Shores, Florida. The small town was quiet, peaceful. And gave a man too much time to think. "If there's one thing I learned from my father, it's that hobbies don't pay," he said to Mortise.

He had a job. A job he wasn't always fond of, granted, but it was a job he was good at. A job he also needed to keep because a hell of a lot of people were depending on him. Harlan Jones was nothing if not a dependable, hard worker, one who took care of those he loved.

His gaze went to the distance, to a hospital that lay fifteen miles to the north. Out of sight, never out of his mind. "I have a job," he repeated to the dogs, to himself, and to the air linking him and the Tampa General Hospital. He best not forget that when he was sanding a leg and admiring the sheen of the wood after the finish was applied. He had seen firsthand where foolish dreams got a man—penniless and unable to support himself, never mind his family. And right now, people were depending on him not to be foolish.

Harlan was about to go back inside and find something else to do with his Saturday when he caught a movement out of the corner of his eye. Here she came. Again. Bound and determined to mess up his life, that woman. "Be good," Harlan muttered to the dogs. "And I mean it this time."

"Mr. Jones," Sophie Watson called to him from two houses down, her blond hair back in a loose ponytail, swinging along her shoulders. From the first day he'd moved into Edgerton Shores, he'd seen Sophie Watson on his daily walk to work. They were pretty much the only two people up and about at that time in the morning, before the sun even thought about rising. She to open her downtown coffee shop, Cuppa Java Café, and have it ready for people wanting an early-morning java, and he to greet them when they were looking for weather forecasts or traffic reports or a quick chuckle as they got ready for their day.

In those early morning moments, Harlan hadn't done much more than say hello as he passed by. Sophie had seemed nice, friendly even, the first few times he'd encountered her. She was a beautiful woman, too, with delicate features and a penchant for skirts. That had intrigued him, made him even consider asking her out. Then he'd found out she lived across the street from him, and that was when the trouble started.

"My dogs are staying on their side of the street," Harlan said, putting up a hand to stop Sophie Watson before she started her daily rant about the twins' tendency to wander around the neighborhood. So they'd relocated a couple of Sophie's rosebushes, and, well, creatively repotted her lilacs and a rhododendron. Oh, yeah, and that incident with the muddy paws and her living room sofa.

Still, Mortise and Tenon meant no harm. They were merely being…dogs. Something Sophie Watson didn't seem to appreciate, as she'd told him at least a dozen times. "The dogs are staying out of trouble, and out of your flowerbeds. No need to come over here and ruin my day."

She propped a fist on her hip. The small white bag in her hand bounced against her upper thigh. "I don't ruin your day."

He took a step closer to her. "I think you make it your personal mission to be sure I'm as miserable as a horse without a tail."

"I do not. I'm a nice neighbor."

A roar of laughter escaped him. "*Nice* wasn't the adjective I was thinking of."

"That's right. I'm that 'lunatic next door.'" She put a finger to her chin, feigning deep thought. "And 'that neighbor from hell.' Oh, and my personal favorite…'that animal antagonist.'"

He bit back a smirk. So she had heard his tales about their encounters. He had to admit they made good radio. Harlan had always had an ability to turn his personal stories into listener experiences. For years, he'd shared the lurid, boring or funny stories of his life, building a career out of those stories. Sometimes, yes, it nagged at him that he had been so open, but his listeners loved it. "I'm just keeping my radio audience entertained."

"At the expense of my reputation, and that's something I take very seriously," she said, her voice hard and low. For a second, he wondered if she was upset about more than a few jokes on his morning show. "I would appreciate it if you would keep your thoughts to yourself."

"I'm a radio personality, Miss Watson. Expressing opinions is in my job description."

"Find something else to opine about." She gritted her teeth, then a forced smile flitted across her features. *"Please."*

He tipped his hat her way, but didn't make a verbal promise. He had a job to do, and a radio station that desperately needed a boost in ratings and advertising dollars. That came first. "So what brings you to my porch today?"

Another smile curved across her face, one Harlan would classify as crafty. "I'm here to find out if you have made a decision yet on my chairs."

That again. This woman was as persistent as a gnat on a horse's ass. "They are not your chairs, Miss Watson. And they are not for sale."

She'd kept coming as she'd talked and now she stood

at the end of his walkway, that one hand on a hip that was cocked a little to the side, giving her a jaunty air. Coupled with the knee-length flouncy skirt she wore and the low-heels that gave her legs a sweet curve, it made a pretty picture, he had to admit. Something within him stirred. Something that hadn't stirred in a long time. A real long time.

Damn. He'd be smart to keep that in the back with the table saw, too.

"Now, that's the dumbest thing I've ever heard," Sophie said. "Last time I made you an offer, you had four chairs on your porch. Now you have six. What are they doing, breeding?"

"I can assure you, ma'am, that they are not."

"Well, either way, it seems you have a problem. And I'd like to take it off your hands."

The way her green eyes were sparking at him, he could think of a hundred other things she could take off his hands besides his furniture. Once again, he added something else that needed to stay in the toolshed. The beautiful but intensely frustrating Sophie Watson pushed his buttons—and not in a good way. He could only imagine the hell a man would endure being in a relationship with her.

"I don't have a problem. Unless I count you." He paused. Added, "Ma'am."

Seemed nicer that way. And Harlan Jones's mama had raised him to be a nice man.

"The way I see it, I'm trying to take a problem off your hands." She gestured toward the chairs. "Two of them, in fact."

"Why on earth do you want my chairs?" he said. "Last I checked, you thought I was the lowest scum of the earth."

She strode up his walkway, as bold as a peacock. Mortise padded over, tongue lolling, apparently forgetting Sophie wasn't in his fan club, especially since that little debacle at her barbecue party. She didn't pay the dog the least bit of attention. Mortise should be counting his blessings. "My opinion of you hasn't changed. And believe me, if there were other chairs in this town available, I'd be buying those. But I want a local flair for my coffee shop and these—" her teeth gritted a bit "—are quality examples of local craftsmanship."

Even though it was clear the compliment had cost her, a swell of pride rose in his chest. All these years, he'd been making furniture in his spare time, and up until now, he'd kept everything for himself, save for a few pieces he'd given to his brother. He hadn't meant to make so many chairs—it was just something about the art of creating the curves that had seemed to bring him a peace since he moved here, and before he knew it, he had more than he had room for. The compliment, coming from a near stranger, almost knocked his boots off.

"Mr. Jones," she went on, "I am offering you good money for a good product. You and I both know those chairs would have a far better life sitting outside my shop being enjoyed by people than they would sitting on your porch, wasting away."

"They're chairs, Miss Watson. They don't live."

Sophie climbed the four steps to his porch and ran a delicate hand along the arm of one of the flat-backed cypress wood chairs he'd made. The exact one he'd placed out there this afternoon, in fact. His best one yet. The way she touched it, he had the fleeting thought that she, unlike any woman he'd ever met, could appreciate the work he put in, the parts of himself that were blended with the wood, the glue, the screws. The dreams he'd once had that still stubbornly rose to the surface when he was transforming a plain piece of wood into something with beauty and use. Dreams, he reminded himself, not a reality he should entertain.

"You can't tell me that these chairs don't live for you, Mr. Jones," she said quietly. "Because they sure look like they do to me."

"You really like the chairs?" he asked, then cursed himself for letting the question slip out. He shouldn't give a damn what people thought. He wasn't in this for anything other than a little stress reduction.

She glanced up at him, and smiled. "Of course I do. If I didn't, I wouldn't keep trying so hard to buy them."

He'd had a good reason not to sell her the chairs five minutes ago. And last week, when she'd come by, and the week before that. But darned if he could remember it now. "They're just a passel of wood and glue," he said, glancing over at them and seeing the imperfections—the slight dent where he'd sanded too hard, the miniscule change in spacing between the slats. "Nothing more than places to seat your...seat."

As he said the last word, he resisted the urge to peek a glance at her curved seat, as she walked around the chairs and examined them. He did not need to get involved with this woman, or any woman right now. He had a busy radio station over at WFFM that needed his full attention. Running WFFM and hosting his daily show consumed his days, and most of his nights. The station had been struggling for years, and when his brother called him after his boating accident a few weeks ago and asked Harlan to temporarily take over as CEO while Tobias recovered, Harlan hadn't even hesitated. Tobias needed him and he would be there, simple as that.

In recent phone calls, Tobias had mentioned that

the station had been hurting lately. Tobias had under-estimated.

Once Harlan got a look at the books, he realized the company wasn't just a little in the red—it was drowning in a pool of debts. Tobias's own income was a pittance, and that told Harlan that his brother was scrimping to get by. Typical of Tobias, he hadn't said a word. Harlan had buckled down at the office and told his brother not to worry, that he'd have WFFM back on top in no time.

Turned out, it would have been a sight easier to wrangle a herd of cats into a horse trough. But his brother needed him both physically and fiscally, and when push came to shove, family always came first. Tobias had to focus on healing his injuries, not his radio station, and that meant Harlan would step up to the plate. *Take care of your brother,* that had been his mama's dying wish. And so Harlan had and would continue to, no matter what it took.

Which was why he shouldn't be getting distracted by pretty women or pretty furniture. Or anything else. Tobias was counting on him to be one hundred percent commit-ted, and not get off on some tangent with some nails and a hammer. Not to repeat the mistakes of their father.

Harlan Jones may be a lot of things but he wasn't the kind of man who let down those he cared about. They came first. Everything else ran a distant second.

"Certainly you won't mind if I buy a pair, Mr. Jones," Sophie said. Mortise sat right beside her, either keeping an eye on her or trying to make a friend, Harlan wasn't sure. Across the yard, Tenon gave up on the squirrel and started watching the events on the porch. "I'm sure the other chairs won't even miss them. They can breed a few more next week."

She was determined. But she'd met her match in the

stubborn department when it came to Harlan Jones. He wasn't starting a furniture business, not today, not tomorrow, not ever.

"I'm rightly sorry to say this, *again,*" he said, wondering why she seemed so damned determined to rid him of a bunch of chairs that he'd built solely as a hobby, "but they are not for sale. Particularly to you."

A gust of protest left her. "What is that supposed to mean?"

"I'm not in the practice of doing business with people who don't like my dogs. And who clearly don't like me." Mortise glanced up at him, and wagged. The dog, apparently, had forgotten Sophie Watson's twenty-minute rant last week when she'd discovered her transplanted rosebushes. Harlan hadn't.

She sputtered again, clearly ready to argue back. Then she paused, and that crafty smile returned. "Then are they available for rent?"

"Rent?"

"You have no more room on your porch, Mr. Jones. And if you intend to make more furniture—or have any more clandestine furniture reproduction—here, then you are going to need more space. And I happen to need something exactly like this for in front of my shop. So, I would like to rent some of your chairs and give you the space you need."

"No."

She pursed her lips. "Give me one good reason why."

"Because."

"That's not a reason at all." She shook her head. "You can't be serious. I've just made you a business offer here. What kind of businessman doesn't at least negotiate?"

"I'm not in the furniture business."

She quirked a brow at that.

"And I'm not negotiating." Or explaining himself.

Mortise stood, his tail wagging, all friendly-like. Harlan snapped his fingers to call the dog back, but it was too late—Mortise had already crossed to Sophie and pressed his body against her leg, his tail slapping against her legs, sending loose fur flying around them like dandelion fluff. Then Harlan realized why Mortise was being so friendly—

The small white bag still dangled from Sophie Watson's fingers. A temptation that had the dog sniffing the air and pressing closer.

"Are they for rent?" she asked again, trying to sidestep the dog, but Mortise moved with her.

"Mortise—" Harlan warned, but it was too late. Before the warning left his throat, the retriever had reached up, snatched the bag out of Sophie's hands and dashed off the porch.

"What the heck?" Sophie wheeled around. "Your dog just stole my lunch!"

Harlan glanced at Mortise lying under the shade of a palm tree and happily tearing into the paper wrapper. "That he did."

"Aren't you going to stop him?"

Mortise raised his snout and chugged back a bite of the sandwich he'd unwrapped. At the same time, Tenon dropped to the ground beside him and began chomping on an unwrapped cookie. "I, uh, think it's a little late for that."

Sophie Watson sputtered. She cursed. She sputtered some more. "Well, then you leave me no choice," she said. She stripped off her sweater and tossed it to him. He caught it and stared at her. By removing the pale yellow sweater, she'd reduced herself to a clingy tank top in a matching fabric. He blinked and for a minute, lost his focus.

It took him a full five seconds to realize she had stacked up two of his chairs and hoisted them over her head, the muscles in her biceps flexing with the effort. "I'm taking these chairs, as repayment for my missing lunch," she said.

"Hey, you can't—"

"I can and I will. Just watch me." Then she swung around, his chairs on her head, and strode off down his stairs.

Harlan glanced at his dogs. "Why didn't you stop her?"

Mortise and Tenon looked up at him, then, Harlan swore, the dogs shrugged before going back to devouring Sophie Watson's lunch between their paws.

Well, hell. Harlan was definitely going to have to do something about that woman before she drove him completely over the edge.

CHAPTER TWO

"NICE chairs." Lulu Saunders shot Sophie a grin, then plopped into one of the two Adirondack-style oak chairs that now sat on either side of a small brightly tiled table in front of the Cuppa Java Café. The handmade chairs were the perfect complement to the homey atmosphere of the coffee shop. She'd been looking for outdoor furniture for months, and when she spied these on Harlan Jones's porch one afternoon, she'd stopped looking at any other types. They were perfect, and even better, made by a local resident.

In a small town like Edgerton Shores, the more local the better. Sophie bought her coffee beans from a local vendor who roasted them on site, made her muffins with local ingredients, and catered to her clientele with drinks named after local celebrities. She'd hired Lulu, who came from a family that had lived in this town for as long as there'd been an Edgerton Shores, and who, with her outgoing, boisterous personality, was nearly a local legend. Sophie herself had lived here all her life, and wanted the coffee shop to feel as if it had been here forever, too.

Which was why she'd tangled with that annoying Harlan Jones this morning. That man got on her nerves in the worst way. On top of that, he had the most incorrigible dogs in the world. And it seemed he was determined to make her a laughingstock in her own town. But he made some seriously nice chairs.

Sophie dropped into the opposite chair and turned her face up to greet the sun. She had a rare temporary break, with no customers in the shop. She spent most of her days here, dispensing lattes and fresh-baked biscotti, and though she loved her job, she also loved the occasional opportunity to enjoy the fruits of her labor. "Thanks," she told Lulu. "I stole them from Harlan Jones's front porch."

"Stole them?"

"Yep. That man is too stubborn for his own good."

"And sexy," Lulu said with a sigh. She pushed her dark brown hair off her brow, and then took a sip of one of the two iced coffees she'd brought out earlier. "Not to mention that Southern drawl. He's yummy all around."

Sophie laughed. "Yummy? I wouldn't describe Harlan Jones with that word or anything close to it."

"Then you are blind, girlfriend, because that man is the sexiest thing to come to this town in a long time." Lulu pressed a hand to her chest. "And since I'm the one who rented that house to him, you should be thanking me for improving the neighborhood view."

Mildred Meyers came striding down the sidewalk, saving Sophie from replying about Harlan Jones's sexiness quotient. Probably a good thing, because Sophie had no time for a man in her life. She'd learned her lesson about trying to mix a relationship and a business that consumed most of her hours, a lesson that had ended her engagement and left her wondering how anyone managed to combine entrepreneurship with a personal life. On top of that, the messy and very public ending of her relationship with Jim had been the talk of the town for months.

Reminder to self: Never run out on your own wedding on a slow news day. The reporters had bugged her for weeks, disrupting her life and her business. Thank goodness the furor had finally died down. Sophie was inordinately relieved when Gertrude Maxwell took up a Winchester shotgun and chased her cheating husband out of the house, thus becoming the new topic du jour.

Either way, Sophie loved her cozy little coffee shop. It wasn't just her business, it was her refuge, even if building the business into something strong and viable was a continual, energy draining effort. She worked hard, but at a job she loved. When she reached the end of her week and realized she hadn't so much as flirted with a man, never mind go out on a date, she told herself there'd be time later for a relationship.

Yeah, like maybe when she was in a retirement home.

"I've had the most amazing brainstorm!" Mildred exclaimed as she approached them.

Sophie smiled. Combining Mildred with the word "brainstorm" could very well be a dangerous proposition. Mildred had once been a teacher—had even served as Sophie's third grade teacher—and had always been an active member of Edgerton Shores. She was an effusive, quirky woman with a penchant for bright clothing in garish combinations. Today she had on a pair of neon-lime Capri pants and a coral blouse that seemed to rival the sun in color strength. A chunky turquoise-and-gold necklace completed the ensemble, and was echoed in her jeweled sandals. "Where's your partner in crime?" Sophie asked.

"Your grandmother was feeling a bit under the weather, so she stayed home today."

Concern flooded Sophie as she and Mildred headed into Cuppa Java and Sophie started making Mildred her usual order. "I should leave and go see her. Make sure she's okay."

"You'll do no such thing. Your grandmother told me specifically that you were 'not to worry or run over to her house for no good reason.'" Mildred fluttered her fingers in air quotes. "She is just fine, and 'you have enough on your hands,' quote, unquote."

"Are you sure?"

"Of course I am. Besides, I left my can of pepper spray there. She's covered for any situation."

Sophie bit back a laugh. Mildred and her pepper spray. Ever since she'd read a newspaper article saying that local crime had risen two percent over the last year, she'd started carrying the little can in her purse.

"Miss Meyers, I hardly think there's going to be a pepper spray–worthy incident in Edgerton Shores this afternoon."

"You never know," she said, wagging her finger in Sophie's direction. "Anyway, back to why I'm here. I came up with the most brilliant idea!"

Sophie finished mixing a latte for Mildred, then slid the coffee over to her. Lulu had also come inside and was busy loading fresh-baked cookies into the glass display case. "For what, Miss Meyers?" Sophie asked.

"For the town's Spring Fling, of course. We wanted something that would draw attention to the town and get people around here excited again." Mildred's red lips spread in a wide smile. "And I've got the perfect solution." Mildred dug in her floral tote bag and took out a thick pad of paper filled with notes in her distinctive loopy handwriting. "A love lottery."

Lulu sputtered, biting back a laugh. Sophie cocked her head, sure she'd heard Mildred wrong. "A love *what?*"

"A love lottery. I told your grandma about it and she thought it was a splendid idea. All the single people in town put in applications to be matched with another single person. They pay a few dollars for their match, and once they find their perfect love, they go out on a date."

"Like one of them, whatcha call it? Online dating services?" Lulu asked.

Mildred waved a dismissive hand, then tucked the notepad back into her tote bag. "We aren't going to do any fancy internet stuff. We'll be matching people based on similar interests, the old-fashioned way."

"What old-fashioned way?" Lulu asked.

Mildred pressed a hand to her ample bosom. "By instinct, of course. By, well, my instincts, since I have so much dating experience."

Sophie looked at Lulu. Lulu looked at Sophie. Both of them decided not to ask about any of Mildred's dating experiences. There were times when a little information was just too much.

"I'm not sure about this," Sophie said. "Do you really think we'll have enough participation? Edgerton Shores is a pretty small town."

Mildred harrumphed. "I have done my research, and this town has a sixty-two percent available rate. We are home to some highly desirable singles."

"We are?" Lulu said. "Someone better tell me where they are, then, because I've been looking for a man for way too long. Specifically, a man with a *j-o-b*."

Sophie laughed. Poor Lulu hadn't exactly gotten lucky in love, though Sophie wasn't one to talk. She'd thought she'd had it all, then realized pretty quickly that was a figment of her imagination. That she'd mistaken infatuation for love and had missed the warning signs that she was marrying Mr. Wrong. Thank God she'd gotten smart before she got a wedding band.

The media, however, had never seemed interested in her side of the story. They'd loved the sensation of a bride ditching her groom at the last minute—and that was all the sentence they wanted before they put in the period.

"For instance, there's Art Conway, over on LaBelle Terrace," Mildred said, interrupting Sophie's thoughts. "That man's got a nice retirement package from GE, and a brand-new Cadillac." A smile danced across the older woman's features. "He's quite the talk at the senior center."

Sophie bit back a laugh. She could just see the results of the love lottery—a whole lot of eligible retirees making a love connection. Chances were it would spur more hanky-panky at the bingo hall than anywhere else. Still, it sounded like a pretty good idea, and an easy fundraiser.

Sophie glanced at Mildred's notes. "It could work. Maybe. But I'm not sure we'd be able to raise the money we need."

"You have a point." Mildred pressed a finger to her bright coral lips.

"Unless…we combine this with the Spring Fling celebration," Sophie said. "That's never a very big event, just a picnic on the town square and a dance at the end of the week. Making it the highlight of the week would increase awareness for the community wellness center. Maybe then all the events combined would bring in more money."

Mildred nodded. "I know how important that is to you. It's something this town has needed for a long time."

For the past year and a half, Sophie had been working to raise money to open a community wellness center to provide much needed services for the town's large senior citizen population. Sophie had proposed the idea, after watching her grandmother's health decline over the last few years. If there was some kind of a community place where Grandma Watson could go with her friends, to take exercise classes, cooking classes, or simply to fill her days with fun, she would. Grandma got out from time to time, but ever since her hip replacement a few months ago, she'd become more frustrated by the lack of nearby venues for a day or night out. The closest place like that to Edgerton Shores was nearly forty-five minutes away—a trip that could double during tourist season. The town needed its own place, and needed it soon. Sophie and the rest of the committee members had held a bake sale, a fish fry and even sold T-shirts, but it hadn't been nearly enough. She glanced again at Mildred's notes. "This could be just the kind of thing that would add to the project's coffers."

"We could put out the word to nearby towns," Lulu said. "There are single gals all over Tampa Bay looking for Mr. Right."

"Great idea. And if we have enough participation in this love lottery thing," Sophie said, running some quick numbers in her head, "we'll be one step closer to building that community and wellness center. Maybe even have enough money to start renovating that building Art Conway gifted to the town last year."

"Art is quite the man." Mildred sighed. "He knows how much this town needs a place that meets everyone's needs." She flexed her right arm. "As for me, I could use a power-lifting class."

Sophie chuckled. "You and me both, Miss Meyers. Okay. I say we go for it."

Mildred clapped her hands together. "Wonderful!" Then she thrust her bright floral tote bag into Sophie's hands. "I think you'll do a terrific job with this."

"What? Me? But I—"

"Volunteered to head the publicity for the Spring Fling this year, remember?" Mildred gave Sophie an apologetic smile. When Sophie had volunteered to promote the annual town celebration, she hadn't expected it to involve much more than sending a few press releases to the local media. And she certainly hadn't anticipated having to promote a date day. "And if you ask me, nothing deserves publicity like a Love Lottery." She turned to go, her mission of passing the buck completed. Then she paused, and cast another smile over her shoulder. "And don't forget, as head of the Love Lottery, you need to participate, too."

"Oh, no, that's the last thing I need. To make my love life public again." The whispers about the runaway bride had finally died down. There hadn't been a call from a reporter in over six months. She had no desire to get the gossips buzzing again. It wasn't good for business and it definitely wasn't good for her. "Besides, I have my hands full already with the shop and now—" Sophie held up the folder "—this."

"Your hands are never too full for love, dear." Mildred toodled a little wave, and walked away, leaving Sophie holding the bag. Literally.

Harlan gave Sophie Watson thirty minutes, then he plopped his hat back on his head and strode downtown, Mortise and Tenon trailing along at his feet, a pair of happy panting puppies ready to go anywhere.

Harlan found Sophie standing beside his chairs, picking up an iced something or other from the tiny table she'd set between the two wooden seats. "I'm here to give you back your sweater, Miss Watson, and—" he plopped himself in an empty chair and kicked back "—to reclaim my chairs."

"You can't just sit there." Sophie snatched her sweater out of his hands and shrugged into it.

"Reckon I can. These are stolen property. *My* stolen property. I'm staking my claim before anyone gets any crazy ideas—" he turned to her and arched a brow "—and tries something like branding them."

"I don't own a branding iron, Mr. Jones, so the identity of your chairs is safe. Though I would be glad to hang a sign promoting your woodworking." That crafty smile flitted across her face. "As an expression of my gratitude for your temporary relocation of the chairs to my front door."

"No need for a sign. I'm not in the woodworking business." Not now, not ever. "And this 'temporary relocation' ain't nothing more than a furniture hijacking. So I reckon I'll sit here until you're ready to give back what's mine."

She scowled. "Those seats are mine for now, and while they are, they're for *paying customers.* Only." The dogs settled at Harlan's feet, with Mortise resting his snout on Harlan's boot. "And there are no dogs allowed in the shop."

"We aren't in the shop, we're outside, on the public sidewalk. And as for customers…" He looked up and down the sidewalk, then peered around Sophie and into the shop. It was just after two, and the usually busy coffee shop was nearly deserted. "Seeing as there aren't many of those right now, I think I can sit here in peace. Should a…what'd you call them?" He smirked, teasing her.

She pursed her lips. "*Paying* customer."

He tipped a finger her way. "Should one of those happen by, I will gladly vacate my seat for the time they need it. Until then, I'm here." He lowered the brim of his hat and tipped his head back, as if he were about to take a nap.

"You are the most infuriating man in Edgerton Shores," Sophie said, and for a second, he was sure she'd dump that iced something or other right onto his head.

A part of him found her feistiness…intriguing. Hell, attractive.

"I refuse to let you sit there unless you are a paying customer," she said.

"And I refuse to let you keep my chairs. They're mine, and I'm damned well going to sit in them. Here or on my own porch, your choice."

"You're really going to sit there, no matter what I do?"

"You could come over here, kiss me for thirty minutes straight and I'd still stay." He'd kept the hat over his eyes, so he couldn't see her, but he could hear her fuming beside him. He wondered if she'd go that far, and for a second, hoped she did.

"It would be a cold day in hell before I'd do that."

"Good thing we're in Florida. No chance of any ice forming around here." From the corner of his eye, he noticed her clench and unclench her fist. He bit back a chuckle. If he'd known it was this much fun to drive Sophie Watson crazy, he'd have camped out at her shop long ago.

The woman deserved every bit of aggravation he gave her. She was always coming over to his house, lecturing him about his dogs, the length of his lawn, the furniture he made. He was pretty sure Sophie Watson had an opinion about every darned thing in the world.

"I can't have you sitting here indefinitely," she said.

He pretended to think that over, when in fact, he'd had a plan in mind before he even showed up. Sophie Watson had been driving him crazy for weeks. It was time for a little turnaround. Maybe then she'd get off his back and let him have a little peace. He had a radio station to run, a brother to worry about. He didn't need the distraction of a sassy barista with a thorn in her thumb she'd named Harlan. "I've rethought your offer of rent."

"You have?"

"I'd be mighty pleased to rent these chairs to you. I'm sure we can work out an equitable deal."

"If it's money you want—"

"Nope. Just a drink and the pleasure of your company." He tossed her a grin, to show her he wasn't all bad. And just because he could see in her face how much it drove her crazy when he teased her. Oh, this was going to be fun. By the time he was done, she'd be marching those chairs back to his front porch and staying out of his way for good.

And in the meantime, he'd have a hell of a story to tell his radio listeners. A win-win all around.

She considered his words for a moment, a parade of emotions dancing across her delicate features. "I'd say that's a fair offer, Mr. Jones." She turned toward the shop. "I'll go get you a cup of coffee."

He popped forward, the hat slipping back on his head and exposing his eyes. "I'd say it is, except I don't drink coffee."

"Everyone drinks coffee," Sophie said.

"Apparently not, Miss Meyers."

She let out a long breath. "What *do* you drink?"

He grinned. "I'm a tea man. Get me a good cup of Earl Grey and I'm all yours."

Her gaze filled with skepticism. "You don't look like a tea man."

"Appearances can be deceiving, Miss Watson. I might even be a nice guy and here you're thinking I'm the devil in cowboy boots." He tipped back in the chair, crossed his feet at the ankles—exposing said boots—and crossed his arms over his chest. Tenon let out a sigh and sprawled at his feet.

"Oh, I don't think it, Mr. Jones," Sophie said as she turned toward the door of the shop. "I know you are."

* * *

"That man is the most annoying human being on this planet," Sophie fumed as she readied the hot water and tea bag for Harlan Jones. This was the last thing she needed. She already had a business to run, a fundraiser to head and a grandmother to worry about. She didn't need to add Harlan Jones to the mix.

"I think he's pretty cute for being so annoying," Lulu said. "He's got that cowboy butt and those big brown eyes and—"

"I've seen his butt *and* his eyes and I am unimpressed."

"You are full of beans, Sophie."

"No, I'm not." The hot water spigot hissed steam as she turned the knob. She dropped a tea bag into the mug, placed it on a saucer, and then loaded that on a tray, along with a tiny pitcher of milk, and some sugar. She debated adding honey, then decided a man like Harlan Jones probably didn't like something that sweet.

Lulu raised a brow at her. "You've been over to that man's house seven times in the past month."

"I have had my issues with him as a neighbor and dog owner, that's why. And because I like his chairs."

"You like what he puts in his chairs."

"I'm not attracted to him."

"Uh-huh."

"He drives me crazy. Him and his damned dogs. Don't you remember what those terrors did to the steaks I had on the grill last weekend?"

Lulu laughed. "I never seen a dog run so fast."

"They were like a band of thieves. One starts digging up my lilacs—serving as the distraction, I'm sure—while the other jumps on the grill, yanks those steaks right off the barbecue. They were gone before I could do a thing. I had to serve everyone grilled cheese." She shook her head. "I bet he trains them to be bad."

Lulu laughed. "They're dogs who spied an opportunity and took it."

"That opportunity happened to be dinner. Yours and mine and everyone else's."

Lulu shrugged. "So give them a biscuit the next time you see them and maybe then they'll leave your lilacs alone."

Sophie snorted. "Those dogs would probably bite off my hand. I like dogs, but Harlan Jones's dogs aren't ordinary dogs. They're…golden-coated monsters." Not to mention, they were huge. The only dogs Sophie had ever spent a lot of time around had been her mother's dachshunds. Energetic, but small, and eager to please. The two Goldens were big and looked ready to topple her at any moment. She'd heard that breed was supposed to be friendly and smart, but Harlan's dogs were rambunctious giants who never listened to her.

"Okay, so you don't like the man's dogs," Lulu said. "What about his voice? You can't tell me you don't like that sexy drawl lighting up your mornings."

"I don't listen to him anymore. You know that."

"I thought he was pretty funny."

Sophie shot Lulu a glare. "He was making fun of me."

Thank God he hadn't heard the story of her breakup. It was bad enough that he recounted their every neighborhood argument on his radio show. If he got wind of the public demise of her relationship last year, Sophie could just imagine how long he'd milk that particular joke. She had no desire to be back under the media spotlight again. She'd be perfectly happy doing her job every day and not worrying about nosy reporters. "Harlan Jones doesn't care about anything but his ratings."

"Oh, lighten up, Sophie. That man could make fun of

me anytime, long as he used that drawl when he did it. He's like a piece of candy in your ear."

"Which only makes you deaf. Honest, I don't see his appeal." In the weeks he had been in Edgerton Shores, Harlan Jones had seemed to convert every local resident into a WFFM fan. Women stopped him on the street just to hear him speak and men dropped by his yard to ask him what he thought of the Marlins or the Dolphins that season.

Every resident but Sophie.

She'd come inside to escape him, but it seemed it was impossible to do that. When Harlan wasn't on the radio, he was on the tip of people's tongues, or worse, he was here. And thus a topic of conversation.

Okay, so he had a nice smile. And a sexy drawl. Didn't mean he was the kind of guy she wanted, or needed, in her life. He was the antithesis of what she was looking for.

"Women on the moon could see that cowboy's appeal," Lulu said, clearly not convinced.

"I can't see why. I mean, I don't even call him by his first name."

"Yet."

Sophie scowled. What did Lulu see in that man? Or for that matter, what did everyone else see? He was too full of himself for her. All confidence and swagger, like he was God's gift to Edgerton Shores. "Why's a cowboy living in Florida anyway? There are radio jobs all over the world."

Lulu grinned. "If you ask him, you'll know why."

"I don't want to know why. I just want him to go away." Sophie raised the tray into her arms.

"Bringing him tea and fresh-baked biscotti is sure to accomplish that."

Sophie glared at her assistant and left the kitchen. Lulu

was crazy. Sophie didn't like Harlan Jones. He wasn't her type anyway. He was obnoxious, rude and mean. And he owned the world's worst dogs.

If he didn't make such darn nice chairs, she wouldn't talk to him at all. Already, she regretted commandeering the furniture this morning. That's where her impulsive streak got her—saddled with the last man on earth she wanted to spend time with.

She had a business to run. A fundraiser to plan. Thinking about Harlan Jones would do nothing but raise her blood pressure.

Harlan watched Sophie come out through the door, a tray balanced in one arm, a determined, no-nonsense look on her face. He could see she didn't want to give him the time of day, much less a smile.

Ah, he loved a challenge. Especially one that drove her as crazy as she drove him.

A twinge of guilt ran through him. He should be at work, trying to get the radio station back in the black. Tobias was counting on him—and that wasn't a role Harlan took lightly. But for now, for just a moment, he wanted to enjoy himself.

"Miss Watson, I do hope you intend to join me for that cup of tea," he said as she laid his drink and some long, thin cookies before him. The water, he could see, was steaming hot, just the way he liked it. The cookies, crisp and fresh. The woman knew her stuff. He might just have to stay a while and make himself at home, considering how tempting she made the place. Surely he could find a way to work and take some time to annoy his neighbor—and all while enjoying a cup of tea.

"I can't sit out here with you," Sophie said. "I have a shop to attend to."

"Seeing as how I'm your only customer, I think you can spare a minute or two to sit with me."

"I—"

"Have you even tried these chairs you're so darned fond of? Might as well plop your saddle in one and see how she rides." He grinned. "Who knows? You may want to rethink our deal."

Sophie hesitated a second, then pulled out the second chair and lowered herself into it. A slight smile crossed her face and he knew, as his own behind told him, that the seat had done the trick. If there was one thing Harlan Jones could do, it was make a pretty good chair. Too bad he knew better than to try to make a living at it.

Once again, the what-if questions flitted through his mind, but he pushed them away. He'd seen how a life built on a dream ended. His father had ended up penniless, with his wife literally working herself into an early grave to put food on the table. What food there had been, that was. Harlan had ended up getting a job at fourteen. He'd handed every paycheck to his mother, and still, there'd been lean weeks, lean months. Times when the temperature on the heat was kept so low, living through those cold winter nights was barely tolerable. And more than one night when dinner was a couple slices of bread slathered with store-brand margarine.

Now Frank Jones relied on his sons to support him for the rest of his days. Not that Harlan minded doing it, but he was smart enough not to repeat those mistakes. His mother had suffered because of her husband's selfish quest, one that drained instead of paid. Harlan would not make the same mistake. And he would take care of his brother for as long as Tobias needed the help.

Harlan shrugged off the thoughts. It was the end of a stressful day. For five minutes, he was going to enjoy himself and not think about the responsibilities that lay waiting for him outside of the tiny circle of Sophie Watson's coffee shop. He could indulge in this oasis, and then go back to shouldering his burdens.

"I have to admit you do make a nice seat," she said.

"Why, thank you. Though I think since you're sitting on something I have smoothed with my own two hands, you can start calling me Harlan."

Pink rose in her cheeks. "You are still a customer, Mr. Jones."

"Technically, you're my customer. And I don't go for all that fancy-schmancy stuff. Harlan will do just fine, thank you." He paused a second, then added, *"Sophie."*

The pink flush turned crimson and washed over her face at the use of her name. Damn. He'd have to do that more often. Just to drive her crazy, of course. Not because she looked so pretty when she blushed.

She half-rose out of the chair. "I need to get back inside."

"What do you do when you aren't serving coffee and…what do you call these?" He lifted up one of the cookies.

"Biscotti."

"Nah. I call them bis-yummy." He bit off another chunk.

She laughed. There. He'd accomplished his goal. She was smiling now. Even better, she'd slipped back into the chair. "I'm afraid I don't do much, Mr.—"

He raised a brow.

"Harlan," she corrected, stumbling a bit over the use of his name. "My business takes up a lot of my time."

"Seems a shame, considering you're living in paradise." He waved an arm to indicate the sunny sidewalk, the palm trees dotting the landscape, the bay's beach twenty minutes away. Like he was one to talk. These few minutes sitting outside were the extent of his time enjoying paradise. In six weeks, he had yet to visit the beaches or watch a sunset.

"Don't you have to get over to the radio station and embarrass someone else?"

He took a sip of the tea. "Nope. I've already done my show today."

He did have a mountain of work he should be doing, not to mention a mile-high stack of financials to review. He also needed to find time to run over to Tampa General and visit Tobias. But right now he wanted nothing more than to soak up the sun. Maybe doing so would clear his head and ease that knot in his shoulders.

"How disappointed your fans must be." Her voice was droll, sarcastic. "To have to wait until tomorrow to hear you bash another human being."

His ego winced at the bruising. "I take it you aren't a fan?"

She arched a brow in answer.

He chuckled. "Well, I guess I'm not everyone's cup of tea." He raised the mug in her direction.

Silence extended between them. They sat there, watching the people walking by. Everyone knew and greeted Sophie, and a surprising number of people said hello to Harlan, too. That told him the show was growing in popularity. Thank goodness.

"So what brings you to Florida from…" She let the sentence trail off, the question implied.

"Texas." He gave her a grin. "For someone who doesn't like to call her customers by their first name, you're treading on some mighty personal ground."

She colored and got to her feet again. "You're right. I'll leave you to your tea."

"Do you often run away from a challenge, Sophie?" If

she wasn't such an infuriating, difficult woman, he might like the way her name rolled off his tongue.

"Me? Run away?" She parked that fist on her hip again. Given how often she did that, it was a wonder she didn't have a dent. "If I remember right, you were the one getting bristly at personal questions. Seems I'm not the one doing the running, Mr. Jones."

One corner of his mouth turned up. "Oh, we're back to that now, are we?"

"I do think its best, don't you?" She gave him a smile that had no hint of flirtation in it and moved her chair back until it sat in perfect alignment with his. A clear signal she was done sitting with him. "Seeing as how we have a business relationship only."

"Are you saying you want to keep it that way? Business only?" What was he doing? He had no time or desire for a relationship right now.

He wasn't pursuing Sophie Watson, he told himself. He was trying to get back at her for her constant rants about his dogs and his show.

Sophie tucked her long blond hair behind her ears and leveled her emerald gaze on him. "I'm a smart woman, Mr. Jones, and I learned a long time ago that smart decisions are the ones that serve me—and my business—best. So the answer is yes. Business only."

Good advice—advice he should take himself. Harlan drained the last of his tea, picked up the lone cookie remaining on his plate, then rose. "Then I'll bid you good day, Miss Watson."

"Good day, then. And kindly remember our agreement." She picked up the tray, added his empty mug, then balanced it on her arm. She flashed him a smile that was anything but friendly. "Because if you ruin my reputation on the radio again, you might get more than you wanted in your tea."

"Is that a threat?"

"Why, of course not, sir." She batted her eyelashes at him. "Just a business arrangement. I'll speak nicely of your chairs if you don't speak of me at all."

"I'll be back tomorrow." He wagged the cookie at her, not making any promises. "But I think I need to up my rent charge. For personal aggravation."

He could hear her sputtering all the way into the coffee shop. An hour ago, he'd been ready to murder Sophie Watson for stealing his chairs and forcing him off his porch. But now, she'd given him a challenge he couldn't refuse. That woman had a breaking point and Harlan Jones intended to find it.

Then he'd take his chairs and his bis-yummy and go back to his own little cave, and forget that sassy woman had ever marched on up his stairs and into his life.

CHAPTER THREE

HARLAN JONES had been coming to the coffee shop every single afternoon for a week, after he got off working at the radio station. Thankfully, Sophie had too many things keeping her busy to give him more than a passing glance. She made sure Lulu had his tea ready every day, but she avoided sitting with him again. He kept to himself, spending his time poring over stacks of documents. He seemed stressed, and she wanted to ask what was wrong. But didn't.

She had no room in her life for a man right now, and especially not that man. The coffee shop consumed most of her time. If there was one lesson she'd learned from her broken engagement, it was that the business wouldn't let her down. Not like a man could.

Despite her misgivings, she'd gone along with Mildred's plan for the Love Lottery. They'd sold matches in the coffee shop and most of the downtown shops, with the big match event scheduled for this evening. Mildred had suggested they hold it at the coffee shop—what better place to hold a first date than a coffee shop, after all?—and Sophie had spent most of the day preparing extra baked goods and ensuring every inch of the café was spotless. She'd had to leave the Spring Fling committee meeting early so she could get ready for the drawing tonight. Hopefully, she hadn't missed anything.

By four that afternoon, when Sophie returned from her last logistical meeting with Mildred and the rest of the committee, she half expected to find Harlan Jones's rear end parked in one of the seats out front. But no, the man was nowhere to be found, and according to Lulu, hadn't been in at all today. Maybe because it was Sunday or maybe he'd given up on that ridiculous notion of sitting in his own chairs and torturing her with his presence.

"Sure does seem quiet around here without him, doesn't it?" Lulu said, coming up beside her.

"Without who?"

"That tall drink of whiskey you pretend to hate."

"I do hate him. He annoys me." She chalked up a new advertisement of specials for the day.

"Uh-huh. Sure he does. Him and that swagger of his would annoy any woman…straight into his bedroom." Lulu winked, then wisely disappeared into the kitchen.

Sophie let out a gust of frustration. The conversation with Lulu had messed up her concentration and she'd mis-spelled coffee. Twice. She took a wet rag, cleaned off the board and started over. What was with Harlan Jones? Even when he wasn't here, he could affect her day. She was going to have to find a way to get rid of him. Agreement or no agreement, she didn't want to find him at the shop when she least expected it. Today she would insist he take money for the chairs and then there wouldn't be any need to have him sitting out there, getting her all distracted.

Before Sophie knew it, the clock was ticking toward six and people were filling the coffee shop in anticipation of the big matchmaking unveiling. Even though she was glad to have the boost in business, Sophie hoped it went quickly.

As soon as she left the shop for the night she wanted to get home to check on her grandmother.

Ever since Sophie's parents had moved to northern Florida for her father's job, Sophie had been Grandma's chief caretaker, and in turn, they'd become close friends. The last few months had been hard on Grandma Watson. Some days, her recovery from her hip replacement went well. Other days, she had too much pain to enjoy her regular activities with her friends, or even to come by the coffee shop for a couple hours.

Recently, the insurance company had cut her physical therapy back to once a week, not nearly enough in Sophie's non-medical opinion. If there was a local low-impact exercise class, one within walking distance of the house, then Grandma could speed up her recovery and strengthen her bones in the process. That was exactly the kind of thing a community wellness center could provide.

Mildred came rushing in, dressed for the occasion in a multicolored floral housedress so bright, Sophie was pretty sure it could glow in the dark. Mildred's gray hair was in a wild cloud around her head and she was huffing from the exertion of hurrying. "Hello! Hello! Are we ready for the big announcements?"

Sophie glanced at the clock, then out over the filled shop. "I think so. I set up a microphone for you on the stage over there." She gestured toward the back corner, where local bands often played on weekends.

"Oh, I'm not announcing," Mildred said. "Why, I get as nervous as a hen in a kitty litter box when I have to speak in front of people."

"A hen in a..." Sophie waved a hand, and gave up trying to translate that particular metaphor.

"You do it," Mildred said, thrusting a stack of sealed envelopes at Sophie. "It's your shop, and you are the publicity director for the project, after all."

The thought of getting up in front of a good chunk of the residents of Edgerton Shores, several of whom had been in the pews at her aborted wedding, caused Sophie's throat to close. "I…I can't."

"Sure you can. You'll be great at it."

"No, I mean, I can't get up in front of people like that. The last time I was in front of a crowd…" Her voice trailed off. She thought back to that day a year ago. The running-out part hadn't been the worst part—it was the stories that had filled the front pages for a long time afterward.

"You ran out on what would have been a disastrous choice," Mildred said. "Those silly reporters just couldn't see the truth."

"All they saw was the fiancée of a man running for state senator 'ruining his election chances.'" She shook her head. "I've never been one for being the center of attention and that…that was far more center than I ever want to be again."

"How are you ever going to get over this little…hurdle in your life?" Mildred said, laying a hand on Sophie's arm, "if you don't just get up there and do it? Besides, you're publicity director. It's your job." She smiled, then gave Sophie a hard nudge in the direction of the mike. That was how Sophie ended up on the stage, calling out names to a crowd of people she'd known since she was a little girl. She stammered and stuttered her way through it, but kept her focus on Lulu and Mildred, making the crowd seem like only two people. Thankfully, the attention was more on the paired names than on the announcer herself.

The matches inspired lots of giggles and applause, especially when Tad Harrison, a cute twenty-something with a cleft in his chin and a ready grin, ended up with DeeDee

Lewis, who had graduated two years ago and still had her cheerleader perkiness.

A roar of approval sounded when Lulu was matched with Kevin Ackerman, a local mechanic who stopped by the coffee shop on a daily basis. Given the way he was grinning at Lulu, Sophie wondered if maybe Kevin's frequent lattes were more a way to see the spunky barista than to quench his need for caffeine.

Good. She was almost done. Then she could get off this tiny stage and back behind the shop's counter, where she was happiest. Sophie let out a deep breath, then picked up the next match, which like the others was sealed inside a big manila envelope. Inside the envelope were two long questionnaires that had been stapled together by Mildred, So far, Sophie would have to say she agreed with Mildred's pairings. For the most part, she'd put together people with common interests, and already Sophie could see several conversations springing up among the newly matched couples. Maybe there was something to this Love Lottery after all.

The door to the shop opened, letting in a burst of sunshine, the kind that came just before sunset, and seemed to kiss the world with gold. Harlan Jones stepped inside the shop, doffing his cowboy hat as he did. He took a seat in the back, far from Sophie.

Was he just coming by for his usual Earl Grey? Or had he put in for a match, too? She scanned the room. Only a few single women remained, and for a second, a whisper of jealousy ran through her that any one of them would end up sitting across from Harlan, listening to his Southern drawl and eating up his smile.

Like she cared what that man did in his spare time. If she hadn't wanted those chairs so bad, she never would have talked to him. He could date every woman in Edgerton Shores and she wouldn't care one whit.

Sophie shook her head, unzipped the envelope with one finger, then raised the paper in front of her face. She hated this—all eyes on her—and felt heat climbing her neck as the crowd waited for her to speak. "And now for our next match," she said, "we have Miss Mildred Meyers with—"

"Mr. Art Conway!" Mildred shouted, getting to her feet and hustled across the room to her intended beau. Art leaned back in his chair, his eyes wide, as if he might make a run for it. Several of the women in Mildred's church group let out disappointed sighs.

Mildred just beamed and dropped into the seat beside Art. "It's like we were destined to meet," she said to him.

Yeah, Sophie told herself, if Destiny was cattle prodded into the decision.

Harlan Jones didn't need a cup of tea. Nor did he need a snack of cookies. What he needed to do was finish booking guests for the rest of the month. WFFM had been struggling for months, and Harlan hoped that by bringing in some celebrities, he'd boost the ratings for the morning show. The ratings had risen in recent weeks, but the sales manager was still having trouble translating that into advertising dollars. In radio, advertising dollars talked—and right now, there wasn't a whole lot of chatter at WFFM.

While Tobias recovered, Harlan needed to increase the revenue stream, using the formula that had worked so well for him in Texas. Harlan couldn't blame his brother's inattention entirely for the station's troubles. The recession, and a loss of the station's top broadcaster who'd gone to a rival station in January, had delivered twin blows to WFFM's bottom line. Now Tobias was recovering in the hospital, his mortgage was three months behind, the station was hemorrhaging money, and Harlan was busy trying to turn the station around to take one more burden off his brother's shoulders.

He cursed to himself. Damn his brother and his determination to do things on his own. If only Tobias had said something sooner, maybe they wouldn't have this mess and maybe—

Maybe Tobias wouldn't be in a hospital room right now. Responsibility for his brother weighed heavy on Harlan's shoulders. Tobias was an adult, but Harlan had never lost that urge to protect and worry.

In their weekly phone calls, Tobias had barely mentioned the station's problems. His little brother had always been upbeat, rarely complaining. It was part of his happy-go-lucky, live-for-today personality, but damn, if Harlan had known sooner—

Well, he would have done something to fix it.

Then Tobias's boat had collided with another during a beer-filled weekend on the causeway. Tobias had fallen overboard, got caught between the two boats, and ended up with a badly damaged leg. Two breaks, and an infection that had kept Tobias in the hospital for weeks. Harlan had come to Florida the minute he heard, and once he saw the condition of the station's finances, he'd moved into the rental house and set to work. He'd realized pretty quickly that his brother had been spinning the truth into butter when it was really melted margarine.

Trouble was, the celebrities who had loved being on the popular Dallas station Harlan used to work for were shying away from some unknown little ten thousand–watt place in Florida. He was going to have to do some serious fast-talking to get any top music names onto his morning show.

Good thing fast-talking was the one thing Harlan excelled at.

As he took a seat in the back of the room, Lulu crossed to him. She moved fast for such a large woman, and had a ready smile and a cup of tea with her when she deposited herself into the seat opposite him. "Well, well, Mr. Jones. You've returned."

"Yes, ma'am." He thanked her for the tea, then took a sip. Harlan had never been one for coffee shops—he wasn't much for paying three times more than a man should for a simple cup of joe—but there was something about coming in to a place that knew your order before you could place it that was well, nice. And, he could look at it as building an audience for WFFM. Whenever he was here, people stopped by to talk to him, offer suggestions for the show, or voice an opinion. It was good business, nothing more. It certainly wasn't about seeing Sophie Watson.

If that was so, then why had his gaze strayed to her the minute he entered the room? Why had he taken a moment to admire her lithe figure before he sat down?

"Did you sign up?" Lulu asked, thumbing toward the stage.

His gaze followed Lulu's gesture. Sophie Watson stood under the small spotlight, her golden hair glowing like a halo. She wore another yellow sweater today—this one a V-neck with white flowers curving around one side—with a pair of cropped black pants. She looked like a human sunflower. Radiant and pretty enough to put on display on his verandah. The problem was that sunflower came with a lot of thorns. When he had time for dating again, he'd be looking for someone nice, sweet. Agreeable.

"So, did you?" Lulu asked.

"Do what?"

"Sign up for a match."

He jerked his attention back to the barista. Match? His brain, overloaded with work concerns, took a while to make the connection. "Are you talking about that questionnaire Mildred Meyers strong-armed me into filling out?"

Lulu laughed. "That'd be the one."

"Then yes, I guess I did."

Lulu sat back and crossed her arms over her ample chest. "Well then, this should be interesting."

"What should?"

"Seeing who you got matched with."

He shrugged, and his mind went back to working on the guest list again. He didn't even know why he'd let Mildred talk him into that thing. She'd stood by his chair out in front of the coffee shop, blocking the sun and going on and on about how this was part of building a good community relationship. Before he knew it, he was handing her a few dollars and answering questions like what his favorite movie was and where he'd take his dream vacation. Then he'd promptly forgotten about the encounter.

"I'm sure the computer they used has me paired up with some nice lady," Harlan said. One date, nothing more. It surely wouldn't lead anywhere. He'd sit here, share the agreed-upon drink with his match, then find a way to beg off from anything more. The chances of Miss Right dropping into his life right now were slimmer than none. Maybe he'd get a funny story or two out of the whole experience, something he could share on the show tomorrow.

A whisper sounded in the back of his head, one that said he'd been alone a long time and he was overdue for someone to shake up his life. Harlan shrugged off the thought.

Lulu laughed again. "They didn't use no computer to make these matches, Mr. Jones, and as for someone nice—"

"We have one last match to announce," Sophie said, holding up a large manila envelope. Lulu stopped talking and turned to face the stage. Harlan sipped at his tea, then fished a notepad out of his pocket and began going over his list of potential guests. He'd come here so he could concentrate—he loved his dogs, but there were times when their barking and squirrel-chasing plumb drove him nuts—and now there was this thing going on. It looked about over, though, and either way, he'd probably missed whoever had been his match. No matter. He'd only signed up because Mildred had been so insistent. If there was one thing Harlan didn't have time for, it was dating.

A hush fell over the room, broken when Sophie opened the envelope. The sound of paper tearing seemed to echo through the room, but Harlan didn't look up. He had flipped out his cell phone and was scrolling through the list of names in his contact database when he heard a name called. His mind, already on the work ahead, didn't process the words he heard. Would it be better to have a top-forty music star, or maybe a music producer, to give a behind-the-scenes perspective of the music industry?

Lulu nudged his elbow, sending his pen skittering across his notebook. "That's you, cowboy."

"Huh?"

"Harlan Jones has been matched with…" Sophie reached in the envelope, then paused and leaned toward Mildred. "There's nothing else in here," she whispered.

"Oh my, did I forget one?" Mildred popped to her feet. "Goodness. I can't believe I forgot to put Harlan's match in the envelope."

Several women leaned toward the stage, one of them crying out, "Me, me!"

"Pay attention, Lone Ranger," Lulu said, nudging him again. "This could be your future wife."

Harlan scoffed. "I doubt that." He picked up his tea and sipped the hot brew. He'd be just as happy not to have a match, and it seemed that was the way it had turned out. Good thing.

He went back to his list while Mildred climbed the stage and took the microphone. "Seems I forgot one teeny, tiny piece of paper. And that's because I wanted it to be a surprise." She turned to Sophie and smiled. "Can't have you staying out of the fun, now can I?"

"Me? But…I didn't even fill out a questionnaire," Sophie said.

"I know. That's why I did it for you. I've known you nearly your entire life, and with your grandmother's help, we got all those questions answered." Mildred yanked a folded piece of paper out of one of the pockets of her voluminous skirt. "And you, my dear, are paired with—" she reached over, grabbed the other paper in Sophie's hand, then held the two aloft, as if they were a matched pair "—Mr. Harlan Jones."

Harlan spat out his tea. Was it too late to ask for a refund?

Harlan Jones?

It had to be a mistake. Sophie stared at the paper for a good five minutes before she accepted the inevitable. She couldn't very well throw a fit on the stage and refuse to participate—that would get people talking about her all over again. That was the last thing she needed—the town and the media focusing on another debacle in Sophie's life instead of on her coffees. She saw the reporter from the

Edgerton Shores Weekly over in the corner, making notes and interviewing some of the couples.

So she flashed Mildred a smile, and acted like it was all okay. Then she'd come down off the stage, and hesitated in the center of the room instead of crossing to her "match." Maybe there was still a way out of this. She'd had enough of living her dating life in public. She headed for the counter, deciding to grab a latte—and delay some more.

"Did I tell you what the committee decided just this afternoon?" Mildred said, coming up to the counter. She grabbed a cookie off the tiered display and plunked down some money. "Sorry you had to leave before you heard the fabulous ideas the other committee members had. Why, come to think of it, it was your grandmother who had this particular lightbulb moment. She called in to the meeting after you left."

Sophie slipped a tiny pitcher of milk under the steamer nozzle and waited while the milk heated, moving the container around to heat it evenly. "What idea was that?"

She'd expected Mildred to say something like they'd decided to run an announcement in the paper that the event had occurred. Or maybe talk a local reporter into doing a little story about how much money they'd raised—not nearly as much as Sophie had hoped, but at least it was a start. Still, at this rate, it would be years and years before they had the community and wellness center finished.

"Your grandma thought it would be a great idea to turn these matches into a media event, and combine it with the week's Spring Fling activities." Mildred grinned. "We've already got all kinds of local businesses on board for the Spring Fling. All we need to do is twist things up a little. It'll be a town-wide dating extravaganza."

"A town-wide dating extravaganza?" All of a sudden

this Love Lottery thing was exploding, getting out of control and becoming a much bigger project than she'd expected. Worse, Sophie was caught in the center of the storm. With Harlan Jones. "I don't see how that's going to raise money for the center."

"We'll have the annual dance, and charge a small admission fee. Host a bake sale, and raise a few dollars that way. Oh! I know. A carnival. Everyone loves a carnival."

"A carnival? How are we going to pull that off?"

Mildred waved off the concerns. "Don't you worry. Leave all the arrangements to me, and you do the publicity."

Publicity? That meant even more media presence. This was the kind of thing that could bring in outside papers…a good thing for raising money, but Sophie's worst nightmare. "But—"

"We need to raise money fast, right? And these events will do that." Mildred wagged a finger at Sophie. "Every penny counts, you know."

"I know, but—"

"But this will be fabulous and it's such a unique idea, we're bound to get lots of out-of-towners and lookie-lous coming by to take a peek," Mildred said, interrupting Sophie again. "Bringing their wallets with them, I might add. So, we were thinking that during something like the lunch picnic on Tuesday, we could…"

Sophie had stopped listening. Her gaze had gone across the room to where her "intended," Harlan Jones, waited. Three other women were hanging around his table, and he was grinning, lapping up all the attention. The man gave self-centered a whole new definition.

Mildred's words trickled through the fog in Sophie's brain. "The couples can share some sandwiches on Tuesday, go to the carnival together on Thursday and then that weekend, we'll top it all off with the annual dance in the park," Mildred went on. "It'll be a week of romance. We'll have to find a way to publicize it, of course. But that's where you come in. You're the queen of publicity."

"A…a week?" Sophie jerked her attention back to Mildred. Spend a week with Harlan Jones? Acting like they were a happy couple? "As in seven days?"

"Well, you can't expect to fall in love in the space of time it takes to sip one of those something-ccino things you drink, do you?" Mildred raised a gray brow. "Who knows. Maybe Edgerton Shores will become the wedding capital of Florida after this. Which you, my dear, will never know if you don't spend some time with your match." She gestured toward Harlan.

"But I—"

"Agreed, as did all the participants, to at least give it one date. Well, I know you didn't technically, but really, how will it look if the chair of the event refuses to participate? That would sure get tongues wagging, and I know you don't want that."

Definitely not. Sophie didn't want to be the center of all that negative attention again, which was why she couldn't understand the logic behind Mildred's match. Sophie, attention avoider, paired with the biggest mouth in radio? The reporter from the local paper glanced over at her, a question on his face. Mildred was right. If the head of the event didn't participate, it would get tongues wagging.

Sophie was all for publicity—if it was for the causes she believed in or for her fledgling business. Just not her dating life.

Mildred waved at Sophie. "So shoo, shoo. And go see what that handsome cowboy has to offer this pretty young filly." Then she headed back to Art, waving a cookie his way. "Art! Oh, Art! Look what I got for you!"

Leaving Sophie with no choice but to accept what fate—or Mildred Meyers—had meted out to her. One annoying cowboy who was grinning at her as if he thought this whole thing was one hilarious joke.

Sophie Watson looked madder than a puppy who'd lost his bone. Harlan chuckled at the glare on her face. She was sitting across from him, her back to the rest of the room, probably so everyone would think it was all happiness and tea between them.

"Why are you here?" she said.

He held up his teacup. "Just collecting on my rent payment. Don't want you to fall behind and owe me a late fee." He gave her a grin.

"I meant here, at the matchmaking event. Why on earth did you fill out an application? Don't you have enough people fawning over you already?"

"Three reasons," he said. "Because Miss Meyers wrangled me into it. Because I like to support the local economy. And—" he lifted his mug "—because I couldn't pass up an opportunity to have some more of your tea."

"I could send you home with several tea bags and you could brew at home. Then you wouldn't have to worry about being here every day."

"Ah, but Miss Watson, it is so much more fun to sit here and enjoy your companionship." He raised his hat toward her, then returned it to his head. "Speaking of which, I'm feeling mighty parched right now. Would you be a good neighbor and chair renter and—"

"Fine." She scowled. "One Earl Grey coming up."

"And three of those bis-yummy things."

"That would require a renegotiation in our terms. I believe we settled on one cup of tea. I only threw in the biscotti because I was being a nice person the other day."

He feigned a pout. "Tea just ain't the same without them. It's like riding bareback on a horse with no hair."

She tried to hold back her laughter, then let out the chuckle anyway. He liked the sound of her laughter—light and airy, like a spring breeze. For that moment, he forgot the responsibilities waiting for him at the radio station, the long To Do list before him, the constant worries about his brother. He felt as light as her laughter sounded.

"And may I assume you have done that, Mr. Jones?" she said.

"No, ma'am. We don't have any bald horses in Texas. But I imagine it's the same as trying to drink my tea without those delicious cookies of yours."

She considered him for a second. "Two footstools, then."

"Excuse me?"

"You want biscotti with every cup of tea, and I need two footstools so people can rest their dogs, as Lulu would say, when they come by. You make me my footstools and you can have your cookies."

"I'm a busy man, Miss Watson. I don't have time to be building—"

"And I'm a businesswoman who likes to make a profit, Mr. Jones. Which means I don't give out my cookies for free." She rose and stood there, one foot turned toward the counter, waiting for him to lob the tennis ball back.

He glanced down at the notepad before him, filled with notes and tasks he needed to accomplish. "I don't have time to build—"

"Then set those breeding chairs to work." She winked. "I'm sure they could produce a set of stepstool twins."

"That they might." He chuckled. Damn, that woman had a way of convincing him to do the very things he didn't want to do. His stomach let out a growl. The part of him that missed furniture building—something he'd had no time for the last few days—said there had to be a few hours left in his busy day to build those pieces for Sophie, if only to get her to smile at him again. In the process, maybe he'd relieve a little of the constant pressure that seemed to linger in his neck every day he sat behind Tobias's desk at WFFM. "Any chance I can get a prepayment?"

"Are you a man of your word?"

"I may be a lot of things that aren't all that good, Miss Watson, but the one thing I am is a man of my word. I say I'm going to do something and I do it. You can depend on me."

"I don't depend on anybody. But I do know where you live, and if you eat my cookies without making my footstools, I'll be by to collect on the debt."

He grinned. "I'm counting on that." Then he met her gaze. "And I'm counting on you coming right back here to eat those cookies with me."

"I have a business to run—"

"Excuses, excuses." He waved off her words. "If I heard right, you're my perfect match." Harlan leaned back in his chair and eyed Sophie Watson. "And that means you owe me one date. Right here, right now."

A moment later, she returned, with a plate of biscotti, and a coffee for herself. She sat down across from him. "So, what do you want to do on our 'date'?"

He could think of a hundred things he wanted to do with a gorgeous woman like her, but none that would be a good idea. "Talk."

She arched a brow. "Talk?"

He reached for a biscotti. "I hear lots of people do that on their first dates. It's all the rage."

She chuckled, then laughed, and he could see her softening, bit by bit. "Okay, so talk."

He waved the cookie at her. "You first. Why coffee?"

"I like…community," she said after a moment. "And nothing brings a community together like a place to eat and talk."

He grinned. "There's that talking thing again. Seems everyone's doing it."

"Especially you, Mr. Radio Host."

"I do my fair share. Seems I got the gift of gab, so I might as well get paid for it." He chuckled.

She sat back in her chair and smiled at him. It was the kind of smile that socked a man in his gut and made him wonder what it'd be like to see her smile like that again. And again. "Well, what do you know? We have something in common."

"We do indeed," he said, trying his damnedest to get his focus back on work, and not on the sweet way her lips curved across her face. "It's nice to meet someone else working a job they love."

"Even if the workload is pretty darn big."

He tipped his tea in her direction, and waited until she clinked with him. "Even if."

"And we have to have similar personality traits to work in our jobs. You have to be personable and know what people want. In your case, what they want to hear. And in my case, what they want to eat."

He took a bite of biscotti, chewed and swallowed. Those darn cookies were about his favorite food right now. "Would you look at that. We're developing a whole list of things in common."

She laughed. "I wouldn't call it a list but it's a start."

"A start works for me," he said softly, then recovered his wits from somewhere around his boots. "For this one date and all."

"Oh, didn't you hear? We're not going on one date.

We're spending a whole week together. The committee decided that the Love Lottery is going to last all week, and culminate with the Spring Fling." She gave him another smile, one that he couldn't read. "So I hope that list gets longer, Harlan Jones, because we're going to be spending a lot of time together."

CHAPTER FOUR

"She's a real spitfire, I'll tell you that," Harlan said into the microphone. He eased back into the soft, worn leather desk chair, glanced at the clock on the far wall and mentally noted the time remaining in his show. "Don't think I've ever had a date with an unbroken filly like that."

His caller—a truck driver named Stan—chuckled. "Sounds like the perfect woman for you, Harlan."

"Nope. I like my women sweet and agreeable," Harlan said. "Like good cooking."

Stan chuckled again. "You and me, man, you and me."

Harlan thanked Stan for calling, then pressed the button to get his next caller on the line. A computer screen popped up to give him the name of the caller and a few words that gave Harlan a preview of what the caller wanted to talk about on air. Carl, who handled the phone calls and kept time for Harlan, held up two fingers, giving him the two-minute warning. Harlan nodded, then leaned toward the mike. "Welcome to *Horsin' Around with Harlan,* Peter. What's your opinion on this town-wide dating thing?"

"It's a good thing, Harlan. You gotta settle down sometime, might as well be with a local girl."

"You looking to get hitched, Peter?" Harlan sure wasn't settling down anytime soon. He had enough on his plate without adding a wife. Still, there were times when he got mighty tired of talking to his dogs and faceless fans. A real person, a soft, sweet woman, now that—

Harlan cut off the thoughts and focused on his caller. Back to work.

Except a part of him was back in that coffee shop, enjoying his conversation with Sophie Watson. Well, enjoying it until the whole date went to hell in a handbasket. And now, he had a whole week of dates with Sophie ahead of him.

He was going to have to hold on to the reins, because he had a feeling it was going to be a bumpy ride.

"I'm already married, Harlan," Peter said. "But I think you should reconsider. I've seen Sophie Watson. A man could do worse."

"Well, this cowboy sure ain't getting yoked to that woman. She'd make my life a living hell. That first date, if that's what you can even call it, gave calamity a whole new meaning. Y'all heard about it. Why, I'm lucky I didn't end up boiled and baked at the end."

Peter chuckled. "If you ask me, it sounds like she likes you. Women only get that mad when they have feelings for a fellow."

"I don't know, Peter. I'd say the only feeling Sophie has for me is loathing."

Harlan glanced at the clock, then cued up the closing advertisements. "Anyway, folks, that's all the time I have today. Join me tomorrow for more of my dating disasters. Because if it's me out with Sophie Watson, disaster's sure to follow."

He signed off, then switched WFFM over to the pre-programmed music that would follow for the next few hours, until the afternoon DJ came in. He thanked Carl for another great show, then headed down to Tobias's office. It was a small room, cramped by a desk, chair and file cabinets, but it had Tobias's spirit all over it. In the mounted marlin on the wall, the photos of him fishing with friends, the sailboat models tucked on the window frame. Tobias had lived a fun life, something Harlan was glad to see, even if sometimes he wished he'd had some of those same opportunities.

Harlan powered up his brother's computer, and opened the station's accounting program. Things were improving, but not nearly fast enough for Harlan's liking. He needed to ramp up advertising dollars, and fast.

He would not let his brother down. Not now. Not ever.

Not again.

He sat back in his chair, tapping a pen on his chin. At his feet, the dogs snored lightly. He could have left them home, of course, but in the last few years, the retrievers had become his constant companions. It was pretty much the only successful relationship he had going, which said a hell of a lot about his life. Things he didn't want to think about or hear, not right now.

The sales manager strode past Harlan's office. "Hey, Joe, you got a second?"

"Sure." Joe Lincoln came inside the office and settled his lanky frame into one of the two visitor chairs. Joe probably only weighed a hundred and fifty soaking wet, but he had more energy than ten men his age. Tobias had done right in hiring him. "What's up?"

"I was thinking, since this dating thing is getting a lot of play on the show—"

"That's because it's hilarious. People love hearing about it. I was laughing my head off this morning. When you were talking about what happened in the coffee shop last night…" Joe chuckled. "Man, you are a brave man to go out with Sophie Watson."

"She's not that bad."

"Not that bad? You made her sound like the devil in high heels." Joe shook his head. "I feel for you, man. And I'm glad I'm not you."

Had he really made Sophie sound that horrible? Sometimes Harlan's mouth ran away from him and his search for a joke went too far. Either way, the show was over for today. Time to focus on other things.

"I was thinking we should take advantage of the Love Lottery with our advertiser," Harlan said.

"How so?"

"Well, so far, we've only targeted the local businesses that are participating. What if we expanded our reach, contacted some of the national dating websites, to see if they wanted to advertise during that hour?"

Joe considered the idea. "Sounds great. I'll get right on it."

"Good. And tell them I've booked Dr. Ernie Watson for several segments and a couple of live feeds from the Spring Fling events this week."

"The Love Doctor?" Joe arched a brow. "Now there's a coup."

Harlan grinned. "He owes me a favor or ten."

"Really?"

Ernie might be famous as the country's Love Doctor, but to Harlan he would always be just Ernie, the same guy he'd known when they were growing up in a small southern Dallas neighborhood. Ernie had gone on to get his degree in psychology while Harlan opted for communications. Ernie made it big when his book on finding the love of your life hit the bestseller lists. He'd become an in-demand radio and TV guest, but he always made time for his old buddy Harlan. Harlan returned the favoring by giving Ernie's books and appearances lots of publicity. They still got together on a regular basis to toss back a beer and talk about the old days.

"We go way back. I helped him disentangle himself from a particularly messy relationship a couple years back." Harlan chuckled. "Seems even the love doc needs a different prescription every once in a while."

Joe paused by the door. "Well, it'll be interesting, to say the least."

"What will be?"

"Hearing what the Love Doctor thinks about your dating adventures. Who knows, he might even say that Sophie Watson is good for you."

Lulu's face, all scrunched up like a puckered lemon, told Sophie she had news to share. And it wasn't good. "Did you listen to the radio today?"

Sophie's stomach plummeted. "He didn't."

When she'd sat down for coffee with Harlan Jones yesterday after Mildred's matchmaking stunt, she'd felt compelled to make the best of the moment, if only because half the town was watching her, along with the local reporter, and she was in her own shop. It wouldn't do to throw a hissy fit and stomp out in the middle—and it would only bring on a news story she didn't want to read. So Sophie had grabbed a latte and a cup of tea, and plopped herself across from Harlan Jones.

Things had gone okay for the first few minutes. They'd kept the conversation light, talking about work, finding they had a few things in common. Then one of his two canine terrors—she wasn't sure which one and frankly, didn't care—planted his paws on the glass of the front windows, clearly looking for his master. Harlan had found it funny, Sophie had told him if he thought it was so cute, he could get out there with the glass cleaner and a rag. He'd called her an animal antagonist again, and she'd told him she hoped he choked on his tea. Then she'd jerked out of her chair, so fast, she accidentally spilled the rest of his tea on his lap. Well, maybe not so accidentally.

End of date.

She'd hoped—no, prayed—that would be the end of it. She should have known better. When it came to Harlan Jones, things always got worse.

Lulu gave Sophie a sympathetic smile. "Your date was the only topic of the day on his radio show. He even said something about how being yoked to you would be a living hell." She shook her head. "And here I thought that man was cute. He's just a wolf in a cowboy hat."

Fury raced through Sophie. That man seemed determined to ruin her life. She ripped the apron off and tossed it onto the counter. "I'm going to march right over there and tell him where he can stick his week of dating."

Lulu rested a hand on Sophie's arm. "Maybe you should rethink that."

"What do you mean?"

"Well, Harlan Jones is making his living off of his little jokes on that radio show of his. Why don't you do the same?"

"Get myself a radio show and bash my neighbor on a daily basis?"

"No. Use this dating thing to your advantage. Get some promo for the coffee shop out of it."

Sophie paused, considered Lulu's words. "That's a great idea. And certainly better than creating another public spectacle."

Lulu beamed. "That's me, a great idea a minute."

Sophie laughed. "Well, in a little while, I'm off to attend

a picnic in the park with Mr. Harlan Jones, so when I return, I'm hoping you have more great ideas where that one came from."

"Don't you worry, Sophie. We'll make sure that Harlan Jones is eating his words before the week is out."

Sophie got busy serving customers, brewing coffee and sending a few more batches of cookies through the oven. When Kevin came in around eleven-thirty, Lulu rushed off to the ladies' room to apply some lipstick. Lulu manned the counter, and Sophie watched her and Kevin pretend not to flirt with each other. A little later, the afternoon help came in to cover for Sophie and Lulu while they went on their "dates." Before she knew it, it was nearly noon. Time to go to the Love Lottery Lunch Picnic.

And act like she didn't think Harlan Jones walked with the scum of the earth.

She stopped in the restroom, then chided herself when she checked her reflection just as Lulu had earlier. Sophie wasn't interested in Harlan Jones. Why did she care what she looked like for a date with him? He was the last man on earth she'd want to attract, and even if she did, she didn't have room or need for a man in her life. She'd learned her lesson with Jim. A man who made his living in the public eye came attached to trouble. No need to repeat that particularly painful chapter of her life.

The early-April temperature had been in the mid-seventies all day, rising now that the noon sun was high in the sky. A slight breeze whispered against her skin, carrying with it the scent of the ocean, so Sophie decided to walk to the town park. Edgerton Shores was a little over fifteen minutes inland from Tampa Bay, which kept the number of tourists down and preserved the town's atmosphere of a close-knit community.

Sophie rounded the corner, and found the town park

filled to capacity with chatting couples. The same reporter from the *Edgerton Shores Weekly* lingered along the fringes, camera in hand. Sophie scanned the crowd, hoping for more media coverage, but she saw no one. Damn. She'd sent out all those press releases, made all those calls, and it hadn't netted the response she'd hoped for. Somehow, she had to find a way to garner more interest from the media. Only then would they attract the outside dollars needed to turn this event into a fundraising success.

Lulu's words echoed in Sophie's head. There had to be a way to make use of Harlan Jones and his runaway mouth.

Speaking of Harlan, where was he? Not that she cared, really, but if they were going to have a date, she wanted it to be over and done before he had a chance to find something to exploit on his show.

Sophie navigated around the crowds, stopping at the picnic area set up to the far right side of the playground. She saw a familiar face, and plopped onto the bench beside her grandmother. Worry fluttered through her at her grandmother being outside in the growing heat, but surely Grandma Watson wasn't intending to stay long.

Since her hip-replacement surgery three months ago, Grandma Watson had been itching to get out and about again. Fiercely independent, she hated the confinement imposed by first her broken hip, then her recovery. She'd been missing Grandpa Watson a lot, and had tried to keep busy so she wouldn't dwell on the empty place at the table. Sophie had tried to encourage Grandma Watson to move into Sophie's ranch house three blocks away, but Grandma had refused. She liked her little bungalow, and liked calling her own shots, whether or not they were doctor-advised choices.

Although sometimes she just up and took a walk—which

drove Sophie crazy with worry—by and large, Grandma Watson would be sure to go out with a friend, usually with Mildred. The two of them were often coconspirators in Sophie's life, both determined to find Sophie's Mr. Right.

"Hey, Grandma, what are you doing here?" Sophie leaned over and drew her eighty-year-old grandmother into a quick hug. "Don't tell me you're meeting your own date."

Grandma Watson laughed. "Goodness, no. At my age, I don't need a date, I need an electric blanket."

Sophie chuckled. "I didn't know you wanted to come down here today. I would have picked you up and drove you over."

Her grandmother waved off the words. "You do enough for me, dear. I wasn't going to call you. It's such a splendid day, I decided to walk here on my own."

"Walk? All the way here?"

Grandma made a face. "The doctor told me to exercise, and so I am."

"I know, but—"

"Don't but me, young lady. It's only two blocks and I did just fine moving under my own steam."

Sophie wanted to argue that her grandmother should take more precautions. Her hip was still a fragile thing, and walking even a block alone wasn't necessarily a good idea. Particularly as the days grew warmer. It may be the first part of April, barely spring, but the sun wasn't paying attention—as the day moved into afternoon, the Florida temps were bumping at the bottom edge of the eighties. Too hot, in Sophie's opinion, for her fragile Grandma. They'd had these arguments a hundred times in the past, though, and it hadn't gotten Sophie anywhere.

"So, are you here with your intended?" Grandma asked.

"I'm meeting the match Mildred gave me," Sophie said. "I wouldn't call him my intended anything."

Grandma laughed. "Well, you never know, dear, where love might find you. And I happen to think Mildred has excellent matchmaking skills. She's been pairing up people for sixty years. Did you know she introduced Joe and Ellen? They've been married for forty-five years now." Grandma wagged a finger at Sophie. "That could be you."

Sophie put up two hands to ward off the possibility. She was in no mood to get serious, or committed, to anyone. The end of her engagement to Jim had been a learning lesson and a half about how impossible it was to have it all—a fledgling business that demanded most of her time and meaningful relationship. The last straw had been Jim's words after the rehearsal dinner—*you're going to have to choose, Sophie, because I refuse to be second banana to a cup of coffee. And in a public career like mine, I don't need people joking about my working wife and her little coffee shop.*

They'd had a fight, and Jim had apologized, but by the next morning, Sophie knew she couldn't go through with the wedding. The blinders had fallen off, and she'd finally seen the faults she'd been missing for so long. She could never marry a man who didn't support her—then or now. And worse, a man in the public eye, who made his living catering to the very media that had hounded Sophie after she'd run out of the church. But she kept those thoughts to herself, because Grandma seemed determined to get Sophie married off.

"So how are you feeling lately?"

Grandma patted Sophie's knee. "I'm just fine, dear. You don't need to worry about me."

"I worry all the same." Sophie lowered her sunglasses and eyed her grandmother. "Are you doing your physical therapy exercises?"

Grandma's nod was less than convincing.

"You know you have to do them if you want to get your hip back up to speed."

Grandma sighed. "I know, I know."

"I can come over there—"

Grandma's short gray curls bounced when she shook her head. "You have enough on your plate, my dear. You already drive me to my appointments, and Lord knows that takes enough time out of your day. Plus you make me dinner all the time, even though I tell you I can manage just fine on my own. Don't you worry about me."

But Sophie did, and would. Once again, she wished she had the money to renovate that building and turn it into a community center. The location, just a block away from her grandmother's house, would make those trips easier—and give her a comfortable place to practice her exercises in between. It would be a wonderful central location for monthly checkup clinics, and weekly community dinners. Not to mention, it would be a great social venue for bingo games and picnics, something the whole town could use.

"I'm going to sit here and soak up some sun," Grandma said. "And you need to go find your intended. So, go. Have fun."

"Okay." Sophie gave her grandmother a kiss on the cheek, then crossed the park. She might as well get this second date thing over with—and as quickly as she could without giving Harlan Jones anything to talk about on the radio. If she put a good enough face on it, maybe he'd even say something nice.

Uh-huh, and Florida would get an ice storm before the end of the day, too.

As she headed toward the gaily decorated booth where the couples were supposed to meet, she saw Mildred. The co-chair of the event was cozying up to Art Conway. Mildred was smiling and giggling like a schoolgirl, which made Art break out into a wide grin. The two of them were as giddy as teenagers. A little to their left, Lulu and Kevin were sharing a blanket under a tree, with Kevin working hard to make Lulu laugh. Sophie smiled. It was nice to see her friends so happy.

Then Harlan Jones came striding into the park, a red plaid blanket draped over one arm, and Sophie's smile faded. His canine terrors trailed along at his feet, tongues lolling and tails wagging. The dogs looked pleased as punch to be among all the people, plants and food. Plenty of opportunities for trouble.

For a second, Sophie considered leaving, ditching the entire event. Probably not a good idea, considering she was co-chair, and her hurrying out of the park and evading her date would undoubtedly be a gossip's dream. She could just see that splashed across the front page. She wanted people to see her as a serious businesswoman, not the girl who ran out on grooms-to-be and dates. So she held her ground and steeled her gut.

Harlan stopped before her and tipped his cowboy hat up a bit. "Howdy, Sophie."

How could he act all friendly like that, as if he hadn't just torn her apart on his radio show this morning? She was about to utter a scathing retort, then she remembered Lulu's advice. Turn this to her advantage, even if it drove her crazy to feign niceness.

"Why, good afternoon, Mr. Jones," she said with as much saccharine as she could muster. She even added a smile.

"Looking forward to our lunch?"

"Of course."

"Really?" He arched a brow. Clearly, he didn't believe her sweetness act for a second.

"All right, everyone, time to grab your partner and find a place to sit," Mildred said into the loudspeaker set up on the podium. "We'll start serving in just a minute. Remember, free-will donations are accepted. And *encouraged*." She leaned forward and eyed the crowd. The people standing nearest to Mildred stuffed several dollars into the offering bucket, then hurried away.

People began pairing off, like ducks in a pond. Harlan gestured toward a shady spot beneath a nearby maple tree. "Shall we?"

Sophie worked up that smile again. "Of course."

He unfurled the blanket and laid it on the ground. The instant the plaid hit the grass, Harlan's dogs began to turn in a circle and settle on the knitted surface. Sophie shied away from their massive paws and bad intentions.

"Hey, hey, this is for people only," Harlan said, shooing the retrievers off. The dogs laid against the tree, letting out twin sighs that spelled their dissatisfaction, but they stayed off the blanket. So they *could* behave.

Harlan gestured toward Sophie. "Ma'am."

"Thanks." She dropped to one corner of the blanket, settling on her knees. Harlan took up space on the opposite corner, and for a moment, the two of them stared at everything but each other, the silence between them thick and heavy. What was she supposed to say to this man, her nemesis? How was she ever going to pull off the facade of happily dating him? One of the teenage boys who worked at Mike's Deli came by and dropped off a bag containing sandwiches and drinks. At the same time, he held out a bucket for a free-will donation, and both Harlan and Sophie dropped in several dollars.

Mortise and Tenon, apparently thinking at least one sandwich should be for them, bounded over and pranced at the edge of the blanket, and Sophie leaned away, out of the line of paw fire. The dogs began to whine in concert.

"You guys are scavengers. Get back, and go lay down." Harlan shooed at the dogs.

They wagged their tails. And held their ground.

"They're stubborn," Sophie said.

Harlan grinned. "Like anyone else you know?"

"Of course not."

He chuckled, then fished in his pocket for two dog bones. He turned to Sophie. "You want to do the honors?"

She moved back, waving them off. She could only imagine the mad frenzy the two dogs would get into if she handed them the bones. She'd already seen what they could do to perfectly good rib eyes. "They'd probably bite off my hands."

"Nah, they like you." When Sophie refrained from taking one of the bones, Harlan tossed them to the dogs, who caught the treats midair, then ran off to the other side of the tree, and started gnawing. "Mortise and Tenon are just a couple of babies. They love everyone they meet."

"Yeah, sometimes too much," she muttered.

"So," Harlan said, draping an arm over one knee, "I think we should get to know one another a little better, don't you? We started yesterday, but we had a bad ending to our little talk. Let's try again."

"Why? Are you looking for some tidbit to exploit on your show tomorrow?" Damn. That had slipped right out. So much for her be-nice plan. She worked the smile up again, hoping it tempered the bite of her words.

"I thought you didn't listen to my show."

"I don't."

"Really? Then how do you know what I'm talking about?"

"Oh, people talk," Sophie said. "A lot."

"Which is exactly my goal."

She bristled. How dare this man think he could use these events—and her life—as fodder for his show? As a way to boost his ratings? Her resolve dissipated, right along with that smile. "Harlan Jones, you are the most—"

Sophie cut off her sentence when Mildred bustled over to them. The older woman's bright pink floral dress swung around her ankles like a bell. "My, my, don't you two make a handsome couple?"

"Thank you, ma'am," Harlan said, sending Sophie a teasing smile that she wanted to swat off his face. "And might I say you and Mr. Conway are quite the good-looking pair, too?"

Mildred blushed, and a titter of laughter escaped her. "Why, thank you, Mr. Jones." She started to walk away, then turned back. "My goodness, I almost forgot the reason I came over here. Sophie, would you be a dear and make an announcement during lunch?"

"I thought you already did that."

"I did, but I think everyone's tummies were rumbling so loud, they didn't hear a word I said. I'd like you to get up there and tell everyone how wonderful this dating extravaganza is. And what a great opportunity it is to build a relationship with another person." Mildred danced her fingers in a little wave directed toward Art.

"Miss Meyers, I truly think you're better suited to that," Sophie said.

"Oh, my, not me. I get positively petrified speaking in front of groups. Couldn't you tell? My knees were knocking like little drums. I'm sure you'll do fine. Why, it's just like riding a bike, isn't it, Harlan?"

"What is?"

"Getting over your fears. You get up, you fall down, you get up again and before you know it, you're riding in the Tour de France."

Sophie didn't agree with that logic. "But—"

But Mildred was already gone, the dress clanging back and forth as she made her way through the crowd. Sophie groaned and leaned back, tipping her face toward the sun. "How do I get roped into these things?"

"By putting your hand up." Harlan chuckled.

"I thought it would be easy. Send a few press releases out, the media picks up on it, and before we know it we have lots of publicity for our events. But so far, the only interested paper is the *Edgerton Shores Weekly*. With its circulation of, like, ten."

He laughed. "You could always come on my show."

"Right. So you can bash me in person?"

He put up three fingers. "Scouts' honor. You come on my show to drum up some interest in this week's events, and I won't say one bad word."

"You promise?"

He wiggled the fingers. "I do indeed."

She considered his offer. Across the park, a cluster of people she knew from high school and the shop were seated together. They were chatting, and one woman pointed at Sophie. "Yep, that's her," the woman said, her strident voice carrying across the park, "can you believe she ran out on her own wedding?"

"Right out of St. Michael's," a second one concurred. The others laughed.

Damn. They were still talking about that day, and it had been more than a year. She even heard whispers of the nickname people had given her after her very public run. Cold Feet Coffeegirl.

No way was she getting on that stage. Maybe she could get someone else to do it. Harlan, perhaps—

No. He'd undoubtedly turn it all into a joke and make things worse. Mildred had refused, and Lulu got tongue-tied just announcing the band that played in the shop on Friday nights.

Sophie glanced at the group again. For a year, her friends had been telling her the best way to get over what had happened was to counteract it with positive steps. She'd thought she'd been doing that with the coffee shop, but clearly, if speaking in public bothered her so much, she hadn't done enough.

And if people were still talking about those dozens of newspaper articles, she hadn't done enough to counteract that damage, either.

Sophie's gaze went to her grandmother, still sitting on the bench, watching the goings-on with a bemused smile on her face. That decided it.

She needed to make a change in her life—and one that benefited the thing that mattered most to her. The community wellness center. As Mildred had said, Sophie was the most passionate person about that cause. That meant she was the best person to encourage people to give.

"Seems I've got a speech to deliver," she said to Harlan, then got to her feet. A wave of nerves hit her, but she tamped them down. She could do this. She would do this. No, she had to do this. "And please try not to embarrass me while I'm up there."

He reached for her hand before she left. It was the first time Harlan Jones had touched her, and when his fingers met her palm, fire raced through her veins. Sophie's steps stuttered and for a second, she couldn't breathe. She wanted to pull away.

But didn't.

"Is that what you think I'm trying to do?" he asked.

"Isn't it?"

"You're the publicity director for this thing, right?"

"Yes." He was still holding her hand. Because he wasn't aware that he was doing it? Or because he wanted to?

"Then surely you can understand the value of buzz. What I say on my show creates buzz. Buzz increases the audience, which drives up advertising revenues, which makes the station more profitable."

"So my life is just part of your money-making machine?"

He let out a low curse and shook his head. "No. It's more complicated than that."

Mildred had gone to the mike and was gesturing toward Sophie. "I…I have to go."

"When you're done, will you give me five minutes to explain?" He flashed his trademark grin at her—the same one that starred on the billboards announcing his show on WFFM. "Please, darlin'?"

Who knew a man could make two simple words sound so sexy? Her resistance melted, and she nodded. Maybe Harlan Jones wasn't as bad as she'd thought. Maybe he deserved the benefit of the doubt. After all, she'd seen snippets of a different man over the last couple of days. "Okay."

He released her, and a whisper of disappointment ran through her. She told herself that was crazy because she had absolutely zero attraction to Harlan Jones. Even if the way he said darlin' made her toes curl.

"Then I'll see you after your speech, *Sophie*."

Her name slid off his tongue in an almost melodic tone. She walked toward the makeshift stage set up in the center of the park, trying to push him from her mind, but not quite succeeding. Surely, it must be the Florida sun, not the way

Harlan Jones had smiled at her and touched her. Certainly not the memory of his large, strong hand holding hers.

Yeah, definitely not that.

Mildred introduced her, then turned over the mike to Sophie. She put on a smile, swallowed her nerves, and faced the crowd of couples. "Um, I want to start by thanking you all for coming today and for participating in the…" For a second, the name of the event escaped her. She was nervous; sure that group was talking about her again. *Get it together, Sophie. Get through this.*

Change. She needed change—and she needed to move past that day, and the ensuing weeks of her face on the front page. The only way to do that was to talk into that round, silver mike. "For the, uh, Love Lottery. Our hope is not just to inspire a few love connections, but to build some lasting friendships." Nervousness closed her throat again, and she stopped talking. Her gaze darted to her grandmother. "And in the process, we hope to raise money for a much-needed community center that all our residents can use."

A few cheers went up among the crowd. Mildred sent Sophie a thumbs-up. The encouragement was enough to push Sophie through the rest of her speech. Albeit, still stumbling a little and with a knot in her stomach the size of Toledo.

"So please be generous with those free-will donations, and remember all the local businesses who have donated their services for this week's events. Also, um, a special thanks to Mike's Deli for donating the sandwiches and drinks today." Another cheer from the crowd. Across the way, the reporter from the local paper scribbled notes onto a small pad. Sophie's face heated, and her heart hammered in her chest. "And please, tell your friends and family, so we can spread the word about all the fun events we have planned."

She glanced down at the schedule on the podium. Just a few more things to tell people about and she could escape this public hell. As she started reading the information about the upcoming Love Lottery functions, she noticed her grandmother crossing the park, her steps slow and sure as she made her way toward—

Harlan Jones.

Sophie prayed for her grandmother to keep going, not to talk to Harlan, because the last thing she wanted was her sweet Grandma Watson becoming fodder for Harlan's morning show—or to get tackled by Harlan's dogs, who had risen and were wagging their tails at the approaching visitor.

"Tell them about the dance at the end of the week," Mildred whispered.

Sophie wanted nothing more than to get off the stage and head off a meeting between Grandma Watson and Harlan. But she stayed where she was, keeping one thing in her mind—the need to raise money for the community center. That forced her to keep calm and keep the words flowing.

She glanced at the group that had been talking about her before. They weren't talking now, so maybe the gossip would die down finally.

"At the end of the week, we'll, uh, be holding a town-wide dance in the town square," Sophie said. "Everyone is invited, whether they're residents of Edgerton Shores or a nearby community, so, please, spread the word. A local band will be providing the music, and Jerry Lawson has generously offered to cater the event."

Her grandmother had stopped beside Harlan and was talking to him. Sophie stiffened, sure his dogs would tackle her frail Grandma, but Harlan kept one hand splayed toward the dogs. Neither dog moved, obeying their master's command. They even ignored the sandwiches and drinks Harlan had laid out on the blanket.

Sophie was about to end her speech and hurry back to disentangle her grandmother from whatever nonsense that Harlan Jones was talking, but people began raising their hands, asking questions about times and places for some of the other events that week. Sophie got tangled in a long discussion with a woman who wanted to make the bake sale into a combination bake-and-quilt sale. It was a good five minutes of Q&A, with Sophie sending several glances her grandmother's way, before she could finally step down from the podium and hurry back to Harlan's picnic blanket.

Thank God. The entire experience had been painful and difficult. As she headed toward her grandmother, she felt a hand on her arm.

"Sophie Watson? I'm Paul Leonard, with the *Edgerton Shores Weekly.*"

She nodded, wanting only to reach Grandma.

"I wanted to ask you a couple questions. As the former fiancée of a state senator, don't you think this Love Lottery thing is a desperate attempt to find another man?"

She drew up short. "Of course not."

"Well, you did run out on your own wedding. I'm sure that doesn't bode well for future dates. Is that why you're participating?"

"Is that what you're going to write? Because that's not true at all. I'm participating in the Love Lottery because I support Edgerton Shores and the community wellness center."

"Uh-huh." He made some notes in his notepad. "And

what do you think about the senator's announcement that he's getting married in the fall?"

She hadn't known Jim was engaged again. The news hit her, then bounced off again. "I hope he and his new bride are very happy. Now, if you'll excuse me—" She didn't wait for an answer, and walked off toward her grandmother.

"Sophie, you didn't tell me what a nice man you were paired with," Grandma Watson said when Sophie reached them. "What a wonderful match Mildred made for you."

Sophie cast a glare Harlan's way. Wonderful match? Nice man? What had he said to her? Moreover, what would he do with that conversation on his radio show tomorrow? She was still fuming from her encounter with the reporter and in no mood to talk about Harlan's good qualities. For all she knew, he was as story hungry as the other reporter.

"Yes, he's charming, all right," she said. Like a snake in the grass.

Beside her, Harlan chuckled. "I'm not as bad as you think."

"Maybe," she said. "Maybe not."

Harlan leaned in close. "We'll talk later. And I'll see if I can change your mind."

A thrill ran through Sophie at the feel of Harlan's warm breath on her throat, the low undertones of his voice. Damn. This man was trouble.

Grandma pressed a hand to her forehead. "Goodness, it's warm out today."

"Summer's coming ear—" Sophie stopped talking when she noticed the beads of sweat breaking out on Grandma's forehead. The older woman had paled, and was trembling a bit. Sophie reached for her elbow. "Grandma, are you okay?"

"Just fine. A little faint, nothing to worry about." She

worked a smile to her face. "I think I overdid a bit today. It's getting so warm out. I think summer is coming early this year."

"It is mighty hot, Mrs. Watson," Harlan said. "Do you want me to go fetch you a glass of water?"

"Why don't we get you home," Sophie said. "And—"

Grandma tugged her arm out of Sophie's grip. "I don't want to go home quite yet. I'm enjoying my day out."

Sophie bit back a sigh. Her grandmother could be stubborn sometimes, especially about caving to her limitations since her hip-replacement surgery. The more Sophie tried to do for her, the more Grandma Watson seemed to resist. "Grandma—"

"I'm fine, Sophie May." Grandma straightened, but Sophie could see the effort in her face. "Besides, I don't want to miss the festivities."

Harlan gave her grandmother a grin, shadowed by the brim of his cowboy hat. "Mrs. Watson, I believe I've had about enough of this heat myself. That sun has near beat me down." He waved at his neck, as if he was hot, too. "What if we bring the festivities to you instead? It'll be twice as fun with a little air-conditioning."

Sophie gave Harlan a suspicious look. Her grandmother, however, shot him a smile. "That sounds like a lovely plan."

"Then let's get you home, ma'am." Harlan bent down, folded the blanket, tucked it under his arm, then put the sandwiches and drinks back into the bag from the deli. He thrust the bag and blanket at Sophie. "If you'll carry this, I'll make sure Grandma Watson has a gentleman escort to help her home."

Sophie opened her mouth to protest, then stopped when she saw how easily Grandma Watson accepted Harlan's proffered arm. He had positively charmed her grandmother—and charmed her into taking it easy for the rest of the day.

Had she been reading him wrong all this time? Was he really a nice guy underneath that radio show?

Sophie gave Harlan a smile of gratitude, then followed behind them, carrying the picnic, while the dogs padded alongside her, stealing glances at the bag of food. "Don't even think about it," she muttered to the dogs.

Grandma must have already told Harlan where she lived, because at the end of the park, he turned right, keeping his steps slow and steady so her grandmother could keep pace. Within minutes, the noise of the picnic was behind them, and they were strolling down the palm tree–lined street that led to Grandma's little bungalow. All the while, Grandma kept her grip on Harlan's arm, and he kept his hand on hers, while he chatted with her about the town. "So, Mrs. Watson, have you lived here all your life?"

"Just about. I moved here when I was two years old. My daddy ran a tile business for thirty years."

"Sounds like he was quite the entrepreneur."

"Oh, he was, he was. Biggest tile business this side of Florida. I worked there when I was a young girl."

"What was that, last year?"

Grandma giggled—actually giggled—and gave Harlan's arm a swat. "You are quite the charmer, young man."

This wasn't the Harlan Jones who had moved into her neighborhood. Or the one who had made making fun of Sophie into a part-time job. This was a man who had an easy, caring way about him, who looked out for those around him.

Who was this Harlan Jones?

And more, why was she suddenly looking at him and seeing him in a new light? And wondering what it would be like to spend more time with him?

"That's quite the accent you have there, Mr. Jones," Grandma said. "Where are you from?"

"Dallas, Texas, is where I was born and raised, ma'am, but right now, Edgerton Shores is home. It's quite the nice little town."

Grandma beamed. If there was one thing she loved as much as her family, it was her town. "It is, indeed."

They had reached Grandma's house. Harlan helped her up the stairs, one hand gently guiding her elbow, while he continued their conversation, as if there was nothing unusual about him helping her into her house. He didn't stop talking until she was seated in a wide rocker in the front parlor. The dogs settled outside on the porch, content to wait under the shade of the roof. If Sophie didn't know better, she'd swear both Harlan and his dogs had been switched by aliens.

Almost as soon as she sat down, Grandma started to rise. "My goodness, where are my manners? Let me go get you and my granddaughter something cold to drink."

Harlan gently guided her back into the chair, then laid his cowboy hat on a nearby table. "Now, ma'am, my momma would be mad as the dickens at me if I let a nice lady like yourself get me a drink I can darn well pour myself. Besides, I have Miss Sophie here to help me so I don't bang around in your kitchen like a lost bull."

Grandma laughed, then settled into the chair, clearly worn out, and glad to have an excuse to stay where she was. "Well then, help yourself. There's iced tea and lemonade."

Sophie followed Harlan into the kitchen and waited until the swinging door had settled in the doorway. "What are you doing?"

"Getting your grandmother a glass of lemonade. If you'll kindly point me to where the glasses are."

Sophie opened a cabinet door, withdrew a trio of glasses, then pulled the iced tea out of the refrigerator. "For your information, my grandmother likes tea, not lemonade."

Harlan took one of the glasses from her before she could pour. He ignored her sputtering protests and filled the container with ice. But he didn't hand it back right away. "What has your feathers all aflurry?"

"I don't trust you." She yanked the glass out of his hand and filled it with iced tea. "Making fun of me is one thing, but making fun of my grandmother is quite another. If I hear one word about you turning her weakness into a laugh for your morning audience—"

Harlan placed a finger over her lips. She stopped talking. Stopped breathing. "I'm not as evil as you think, Sophie."

Damn. There was her name again, rolling right off his tongue. She wanted to hear him say it again. Wanted him to murmur her name against her lips. Just…wanted.

"I don't believe you," she said, but her words were lacking in punch. Every ounce of her was acutely aware of his fingertip against her mouth, of the woodsy notes of his cologne, of the deep blue of his eyes, no longer shaded by his hat, but instead framed by his dark brown waves.

"Why don't you give me a fair chance? Treat this week like a real date. Let me court you—"

"Nobody says that anymore."

"I say it," he said, his words strong, determined. "Let me court you, and see if you still think I'm the devil's cousin after that."

She took in a deep breath when he lowered his hand. Harlan watched her chest rise and fall, then his gaze zeroed back on hers. He had the bluest eyes she'd ever seen—as blue as the ocean on a bright summer day—and for a second, she got lost in that mysterious sea. "I…" She let the sentence trail off, because she didn't know how to end it.

A grin quirked across his face and he leaned in closer. So close, she wondered if he was going to kiss her. Hoped he would.

The moment held between them. Her heart beat. Once, twice. And still Harlan didn't move. She found herself leaning, ever so slightly, toward him, wondering, even as she knew she shouldn't, if he would kiss in the same sexy, slow way he talked.

Only a breath separated them, and Sophie knew if she leaned in just a millimeter closer, they would kiss.

"I'm not as bad as you think," he whispered, his words warm against her skin.

A ploy. That's what it was, Sophie told herself. A ploy to get her to trust him so that then he could turn around and use the encounter to boost his ratings.

But oh how she wanted to believe different. Wanted to let Harlan Jones get closer. Much closer.

"And you're not as good as I think, either," she said, then spun around and left the kitchen before Harlan Jones could wrap her in that cowboy spell again.

CHAPTER FIVE

HARLAN had done hundreds of radio shows. Had dozens of guests in his studio. And had never been as nervous as he was this morning.

Sophie Watson gave him a little wave outside the glass booth. He gestured for her to come inside, then dropped his headphones to his neck. "Perfect timing. I'm on a commercial break for the next sixty seconds."

"I brought you some tea." She laid an insulated cup before him. The Cuppa Java Café logo danced around the perimeter of the dark blue mug, a cute and friendly advertisement. Sophie held a second, matching cup, one that had seen much use. "Uh, where should I…?"

"Oh, sorry." He jerked to his feet, sending his chair flying back a few feet. His headphones yanked him back, and he pulled them off, tossing them to the counter. As he came around the circular counter, he knocked over a mike and a stack of papers. Could he be more of an idiot? He was never nervous like this. What was it about this woman? "Right here," he said, gesturing toward the opposite chair. "There's a pair of headphones for you, too. Just put them on and you can hear me and the whole show."

She sat down, putting her coffee beside her. She slid the headphones over her head, then leaned forward. "And I just talk into this?"

"Yep." He settled in his own chair and slid on the head-phones. "It's easy."

She let out a short laugh. "Easy for you to say. You do this all day. I'd feel much more comfortable behind the counter at the café, steaming some milk."

"Life is all about stepping out of your comfort zone, darlin'." The music for the advertisement break began to wind to an end. Harlan put up a finger to signal Sophie to be quiet, then he slipped back into place at the other mike. "Welcome back to *Horsin' Around with Harlan,* folks. I've got a special guest in studio with me today. Miss Sophie Watson, the owner of Cuppa Java Café. And the head of the Love Lottery." He drew out the last two words, saw a flash of annoyance cross her face. He grinned at her, to show he wasn't all bad. "Welcome to the show, Sophie."

"Uh, thanks." She leaned in so close to the mike, she nearly kissed it. Harlan bit back a chuckle. "Uh, s-s-sorry."

"Sophie, why don't you tell us a little about the Love Lottery?"

Her eyes widened with panic. "Uh, now?"

He chuckled. "Now would be a great time."

She opened her mouth, closed it. Her gaze fastened on the microphone, and she backed up a bit, as if it might bite. She seemed frozen, and a second, then another, of dead air ticked by.

He remembered the speech she'd given in the park—and how nervous she'd seemed that day. Had inviting her into the studio been a mistake? Clearly, Sophie Watson didn't like speaking in public. Why had he thought the radio would be any different?

Another second of dead air—the worst thing that could happen to a radio show—passed. Tension curled in Harlan's gut.

Then he had a brainstorm. "Sophie, why don't you tell me about the charity that the Love Lottery will benefit. I heard it's a great one."

Her features relaxed, her shoulders lost their tension and a smile flitted across her face. "All proceeds from this week's events go toward building a community wellness center. We already have a space, but we need funding to renovate, furnish and staff it."

"That sounds like something this town needs."

"We do. One thing people in this town have been asking for is a place where they can go to take exercise classes, hold bingo nights, and community suppers. We're hoping the wellness center brings Edgerton Shores in new ways, and gives everyone a home away from home."

That was it. When he tapped into her passion, Sophie opened up and lost her nervousness about speaking. It was as if she forgot what paralyzed her and just let go. "Tell me more," he said.

And for the next five minutes, Sophie did. She talked about her grandmother, about how her declining health had been the inspiration behind the project. She talked about the community, about the contributions of everything from a penny to a hundred-dollar bill that had been dropped into the jar on the counter at Cuppa Java. She talked about the center's flexibility, about how it could become something for everyone.

Harlan listened, caught in the fervor in her voice, the animation in her features. He'd known Sophie Watson for nearly two months, and never seen her so energized before. It gave him a new perspective on her—and made him wonder if maybe he'd only been seeing what he wanted to see in the last few weeks.

Too quickly, the segment came to an end. Harlan

thanked Sophie for coming on the show, then switched the programming to music. "That went fabulous. Thanks."

Her smile shook on her face. "You really think so? I think I rambled."

"It was a good ramble." He grinned. "Believe me, if you'd been boring, I would have cut you off."

"Dragged me right out of there?"

He laughed. "Absolutely." Through the glass, he saw Carl signal that he was stepping out for a while. That left him and Sophie alone.

In a small room.

With nothing to distract them anymore.

She ran a finger along the counter. "I'm surprised you do this job."

"Why? Am I terrible at it?"

"No, really, you're great. It's just your furniture is so amazing that I'm surprised you don't go into business doing that instead."

He scowled. "I'm not the entrepreneurial type."

"I never thought I was, either, until I made the leap. I think if you're passionate about something, that makes being your own boss a lot more enjoyable."

"I enjoy this job."

But did he really? Hadn't he had that been-there, done-that feeling lately? He shook off the thoughts. He didn't need to be getting sidetracked by things that weren't going to happen.

"I just thought..." She shrugged and didn't finish the sentence.

"Just thought what?"

"That you're the last person I would expect to be working the nine-to-five kind of job. Especially when you have so much creativity."

"Yeah, well, it can be hard to make a living off of

creativity." Hadn't he learned that lesson firsthand? He didn't need to live it again to drive that maxim home. He'd already seen where selfishly pursuing dreams instead of dependable income got a man. And right now, his family was depending on him. That was something he wasn't going to explain to Sophie, or anyone else.

Even if her comments gave him a flash of pride, and sent his mind down that what-if path for a second.

"Anyway, thank you again," he said. Hoping she'd leave. Hoping she wouldn't.

"No, thank *you,* Harlan. I appreciate you letting me get the word out. And for not bashing me on the air."

A twinge of guilt flickered inside him. "Darlin', you gotta know I was only joshing. I don't really think you're that terrible."

"You don't?" The words came out soft, almost…vulnerable.

He stepped closer to her, even as he told himself not to, told himself he didn't have time or room for a woman in his life. He reached up, and cupped her jaw, his gaze locked on hers. Damn. She had about the greenest eyes he'd ever seen. "Not at all. I'm just doing a job, playing a character. I don't really think that about you."

She opened her mouth as if she was going to reply, but didn't say anything. He stared at her parted lips, desire pounding in his veins, and wondered if she would be as passionate in bed as she'd been on his radio show.

He wanted to know that answer. Now.

He leaned in and traced her bottom lip with his thumb. Everything inside him whispered only one message: *kiss her.*

"You are…distracting," he said. "And tempting."

What the hell was he doing? He needed to get a grip. To get focused again.

The first song ended, and a commercial for a bank came on, sending a karmic reminder to Harlan. Concentrating on the beautiful Sophie Watson meant not concentrating on business.

Which in the end, meant letting down Tobias.

"I'm sorry," he said, and stepped away from her. He turned toward the counter, picked up a sheaf of papers and rifled through them without seeing a word on the pages. "Uh, thanks again for coming in today."

Confusion washed over her face, then she colored, and anger flashed in her eyes. "You're welcome. I'll get out of your hair now." Then she turned on her heel and left.

Leaving Harlan to do what he should have been doing all along—get back to work.

It took three hours of sawing, nailing and sanding in his garage woodshop before Harlan had worked the morning out of his system. The dogs had curled up in one of the shadowed corners, snoring lightly while they waited for their master to stop taking out his frustrations on a sheet of plywood.

Sophie Watson. Who'd have thought that woman could so easily get under his skin? He'd been so sure, when they'd been paired up by Mildred, that it would become an epic disaster. Especially given the way that first date had ended.

He hadn't expected to care about her. To wonder what made her tick. No, she'd simply been a means to an end—a topic of discussion on his show, something he could forget the minute the microphone was off. But she'd lingered in his mind, as stuck there as a piece of gum on the bottom of his shoe. Only sweeter. And definitely less annoying. But still a distraction he didn't need.

He'd spent the rest of his morning at the hospital with

Tobias. His brother had been in good spirits, talking about going home soon, but guilt had fallen on Harlan's shoulders anyway. Guilt that he hadn't been here before the accident. Guilt that he hadn't done more to boost the station in the weeks since. And most of all, guilt that he had let Tobias down all those years ago. Maybe if he hadn't—

Harlan hammered another shelf into the bookshelf he had started constructing. He drove the hammer too hard and too fast, and the wood splintered, cracking apart with a groan and a creak. "Damn!"

The dogs jerked awake, saw there was no emergency and went back to their nap.

"Am I interrupting?"

He spun around at the sound of Sophie's voice. Good thing he'd stopped hammering or he might have driven his thumb into the joint instead of a nail. "No, not at all." A lie. She *was* interrupting his attempts at forgetting she existed. Considering he hadn't made it more than five seconds without thinking about her, those attempts weren't going so well.

"I just wanted to thank you again for this morning. And for yesterday, with my grandmother." She stood in the doorway of the garage, partly in shadows, partly lit by the sun from behind. Her hair was tinged with gold, the sun's rays dancing on the blonde curls that framed her face.

Well, darn. He put down the hammer before he accidentally took out an eye or something.

"It was nothing, really."

She stepped inside, and the shadows dropped away, leaving her bathed in the soft white lights of the garage. "It was a big deal, bigger than you know. Ever since my parents moved away, it's just been Grandma and me. I worry about her all the time, but she can be so stubborn and not ask for help when she needs it. She's independent and feisty—"

"Like someone I know." Harlan grinned.

"Maybe," she conceded softly. "Anyway, I…" She paused, and he could see it wasn't easy for her to be nice to him, which nearly made him chuckle. "I appreciate it."

He shrugged. "Truly, nothing more than one neighbor helping another."

"Well, given our history, I hadn't expected you to be…" Her voice trailed off as if she was searching for the right words.

"Nice?" Now he did chuckle. "I told you, I'm not nearly as awful as you think."

Her gaze met his and another smile curved across her face. This one was the kind of smile that hit a man in the solar plexus and made him wonder if maybe he'd been missing something that was right under his nose.

"Maybe not," she said softly, and the smile widened.

"And I want to say, I do feel bad about the plants my dogs dug up," Harlan said, his mouth running like a over-filled stream because a part of him wanted nothing more than to see her smile again. "I know I replaced them and all, but I feel like maybe I should do something else for you, you know, as a way to repay you for the aggravation."

"Really?"

"Sure, name your favor." Here he went again. Getting more wrapped up with this woman.

She considered his words for a second. "A favor besides the footstools you owe me?"

The footstools. He'd forgotten all about that promise, with the busy schedule he'd been keeping at the radio station, and now the added commitment of the Love Lottery events. For a man who didn't want to be employed as a woodworker, he sure as hell kept getting asked to build stuff. If he was smart, he'd shut the doors of the woodshop and stick to the job he did best—the one his brother was counting on him to do. "I'll have those for you soon, long as you make me a promise."

"What's that?"

"You don't tell anyone who built them. The last thing I need is people showing up on my doorstep, wanting tables and chairs."

"But—"

"That's the deal. Take it or leave it." He'd build the footstools, and that would be it. Nothing more would come out of this garage.

She worried her bottom lip, something he noticed she did when she wanted to say something, and was debating whether she should. "Okay, I'll take it."

"Good." He leaned against his workbench and crossed his arms over his chest. His gaze traveled down the length of Sophie's lithe frame, lingering on the curve of her hips, the length of her legs, the heart-shaped muscles in her calves.

"You mentioned a favor?"

Harlan jerked his attention back to the topic at hand. Better that than thinking about what it would be like to kiss Sophie Watson. "Uh, yes, a favor. To make up for your torn-up rosebushes. What can I do for you, darlin'?"

She worried that lip again, then let out a long breath. "Stop talking about me on your show. Except for a plug or two for the coffee shop. I'd really appreciate that."

"A little free advertising?"

She smiled again, and his gut took another hit. "It's cheaper than replacing my landscaping, isn't it?"

"I reckon so. And I promise, I won't tell tall tales about you on my show anymore."

"Really?"

"Really. Sometimes I forget that my mouth can be a

dangerous weapon." He cleared his throat before he took that innuendo any further. "And, I'd be glad to throw in a plug or two." He pushed off from the workbench and took a few steps closer to her. "Business down?"

"Let's just say it could be better."

"What you need is an event," Harlan said. "Something big, get the public's attention."

She laughed and shook her head. "The last thing I need is more events to handle. I've already got my hands full."

The double entendre sent his pulse into overdrive. His gaze skimmed her curves again, and for the second time in one week, he wondered what it would be like to kiss Sophie Watson. "Hands full, huh?"

She colored. "I meant, uh, busy."

He liked seeing her flustered. Liked seeing her a little off center. It made Sophie Watson a hell of a lot more interesting.

The dogs got up, apparently sensing the break in the conversation, and scrambled over to Sophie's side before Harlan could stop them. Mortise and Tenon, excited at having a guest, jerked up on their back paws, preparing to pounce on Sophie and express their canine love. "Hey, guys, don't—"

But he was too late. Just as he spoke, a car pulled into the driveway, and the retrievers, thrilled at the prospect of even more company, abandoned their greeting of Sophie mid-jump to turn for the small sedan. Their paws bounced off her chest, and she teetered, then just as Harlan was reaching for her, Sophie toppled onto the hard concrete floor. The dogs took off, barking and scrambling over each other.

Harlan stepped around the table saw, bent down and

put out his hand to pull Sophie up. She scowled at him, and ignored his help. "Your dogs are—"

"One hell of a greeting!" The loud, booming male voice echoed in the garage's interior. Mortise and Tenon joined in with a chorus of barking, running back into the garage, and clambering all over Sophie again. As Harlan took in the chaotic scene before him, he realized the détente he thought he had built with Sophie Watson was about to explode into an all-out war.

Sophie got up off the floor, ignoring Harlan Jones's outstretched hand. She brushed the dirt off her skirt, and was about to leave when a boisterous man in a bright red shirt and a heart-patterned tie hurried up to her. He grabbed her arm, even though she was already standing, as if he thought she might topple back all over again.

"Well, hello!" he said, his voice as bright as his shirt. "Harlan's dogs sure love you."

Sophie snorted, and sent a glare Harlan's way. "Love me? They just tried to kill me."

As if understanding her words, the two retrievers lowered their heads and slunk over to Harlan's side. "Sorry, darlin'. I think my dogs could use a little *more manners*." Harlan gave the dogs an annoyed glance, but they had already forgotten the error of their ways and just swatted him with happy tails.

She brushed a little more concrete dust off the front of her skirt. "That's not my idea of liking someone. I should call Animal Control on these beasts."

Beside her, Harlan bristled. "Hey, my dogs aren't that bad."

The man in the red shirt chuckled. "Forgot to introduce myself." He thrust out his hand to her. "Ernie Watson, the

Love Doctor. In other words, an expert in the realm of all things love."

"The Love Doctor?"

"Yep. The very one." He shook Sophie's hand vigorously, then released her. "And between you and me—" he leaned in close, lowered his voice to a loud whisper "—given the state of Harlan's dates lately, I think he needs my expertise."

She spun toward Harlan. "You called in a guy known as the Love Doctor? Why?"

Ernie leaned in close to Sophie. "Why, to help him woo the lady, of course. From what Harlan tells me, she's been a tad difficult—"

"Ernie—"

The other man just kept on talking, ignoring Harlan's attempt to interrupt. "But I'm sure with a little help and advice from the Love Doc, she'll come around and see that my friend Harlan here is nothing but a big old soft-hearted cowboy—"

"Ernie!"

"Now hold on a minute, Harlan, I'm just pointing out your best features." Ernie turned back to Harlan. "This boy here, why, he's the kind of catch every woman wants. Give that little lady some time, and she'll see that, and be all over him with kisses and hugs. Nothing makes for great talk radio like a happily ever after ending. That's why I'm here, so the listeners get what they want."

The words took a long moment to sink in. Sophie stood there, hearing what Ernie had said, looking from him to Harlan. As Harlan's face dropped from a grin into a guilty smirk, Sophie realized she'd been had, once again, by the charming cowboy.

"How dare you?" she said, striding up to Harlan. "Is this all just some marketing ploy? Were you just using my grandmother as a way to get close to me? And what about having me on this morning? Was all that just something to exploit on your show?"

"Of course not. I genuinely—"

"Nothing about you is genuine. I can't believe I fell for that chivalrous cowboy act." She parked her fists on her hips. "Do me a favor and don't show up for the rest of our dates. I think even the Love Doctor here would tell you that you are fighting a losing battle."

Then she turned on her heel and headed out of the garage. Harlan's dogs tried to keep pace with her for a little while, but at the end of the driveway, Sophie turned back and gave the dogs a glare.

Instead of skulking away, the dogs bounded off in tandem—across the street and straight onto Sophie's lawn—and right into the middle of the flowers she'd planted yesterday morning. In a two-second span of time, their eight massive paws turned the bright swath of impatiens into a muddy, pink mess.

"Mortise! Tenon! Get back here!" Harlan yelled.

The dogs did as he said, charging back across the street, and stopping only to leap onto Sophie again, leaving twin dark brown pawprints across the front of her shirt. She let out a curse. "You don't need a Love Doctor, Harlan Jones," she called down his driveway. "You need obedience school!"

CHAPTER SIX

THE picture held center court on the front page of the *Edgerton Shores Weekly*. Him and Sophie talking, unaware of the photographer who had snapped their picture. Harlan had tried three times to throw the paper out, and kept coming back to Sophie's smile.

There was another side to this woman, he'd realized, particularly after meeting her grandmother and seeing the tender, protective way she watched over the older lady.

That was something Harlan could understand, and appreciate. For as long as he could remember, he'd been the caretaker for his family. As soon as he was old enough to work, he'd gotten a paper route, then a job as a janitor at a radio station, working his way up the ladder there while he went to school.

Harlan's father had been unavailable—trying to eke out a living with the photography studio he'd fashioned out of a spare bedroom. He was convinced all it took was one great job and they'd be rich. That great job never came. And meanwhile, his family starved, and young Harlan worked every spare moment he had, helping his mother put food on the table.

Now Harlan was trying to save the sinking ship of WFFM for his brother, taking care of his family all over again. He owed Tobias that much. At least.

Harlan flipped the newspaper over so that the picture was out of his sight, and pulled up a copy of the show's schedule. He clicked through the time blocks in his computer, reviewing the scheduled advertisements and news breaks. Joe had done his job, and booked several thirty-second spots from a national online dating site. Finally, things were looking up at WFFM.

He heard a soft knock on the office door. He glanced up to see his younger brother standing in the doorway. "Hey, what are you doing here?"

"Just saying hi. This morning, I was given a bunch of meds and instructions, then kicked out of the hospital. Seems I'm good to recover on my own," Tobias said with a grin. He entered the room, using a pair of crutches to help him navigate with one leg in a cast, and sat in one of the two visitors' chairs. Tobias was younger by three years, and a little leaner than Harlan. He had the same blue eyes, and the dark wavy hair that was a Jones family trademark. Unlike Harlan, who let his grow until it peeked out from under the Stetson, Tobias kept his hair close-cropped. "I'm here to make sure you ain't getting too comfortable."

"As boss man?" Harlan laughed. "Never. I'm better being the talent than the brains."

"Oh, I don't know about that. You're good at a lot of things." Tobias patted the arms of the chair. "View's a little different from this side of the desk."

"You'll be back over here before you know it." Harlan's gaze swept over Tobias's face. His younger brother was still a little pale, and looked like he could use a good steak. "How are you feeling? You sure you should be here? Maybe you should go home. Take a nap or something."

"My God, you are like a mother hen." Tobias leaned forward. "I'm fine, big brother. Stop worrying. I mean it."

"It's part of my job."

"Speaking of jobs…" Tobias leaned back in the chair and let out a breath. "I want to come back to work. Now before you object, the doc has cleared me to work part-time, long as I don't go running marathons in my time off. I'm going stir-crazy doing nothing, Harlan. Hell, just yesterday, I caught myself watching the Cooking Channel, for God's sake."

Harlan laughed. "The Cooking Channel? You don't cook."

"I know." He threw up his hands. "I spend any more time lying around like a bump on a log, and I'll end up buying porcelain dolls on the shopping channel."

Harlan laughed, then let out a long breath. "Tobias, you know you're welcome here anytime. I mean, this place is your baby. But—"

"Don't but me. I need to work. And I can take some of the work off your shoulders."

"I'm fine."

"Is this about what happened five years ago?"

Five years ago—when Tobias had come to Harlan and asked him to support his then fledgling radio station. Harlan, too wrapped up in his own bustling career, had said no.

Now look where they were. Harlan's gaze returned to the computer. "Of course not. It's about today. Me trying to help you out."

"Bullshit. You'll work yourself into the grave before you ask for a helping hand."

"I'm not that bad."

Tobias sighed. "You don't have to do it all, you know."

"I'm not."

Tobias looked like he might say something else, then shook his head. "Well, one thing's for sure. You're a master at this business. Stupid me didn't ask for help until the EMTs were hauling me off the boat."

A shudder of dread ran through Harlan at the thought of how close he'd come to losing Tobias. If only he'd been here. "All the more reason why you should take it easy."

"I've learned my lessons, big brother. Have you?"

"What are you talking about?"

"Don't get me wrong. I'm sure as hell grateful that you stepped into my boots. But I know how you are. You'll keep on wearing those boots, even if it means you forget about your own."

"What's that supposed to mean?"

"Are you dating anyone right now?"

"Tobias, I don't have time for that."

Tobias put a hand toward Harlan. "Proves my point. You should be able to find a balance. And the problem with you, is you are an all-or-nothing guy."

"I have a balance."

Tobias crossed his arms over his chest. "Oh, yeah? How much furniture is filling that rental house of yours?"

"That doesn't mean anything."

"You build when you're stressed. You build when you're overwhelmed. You build when you're looking for something you can't find. And I ain't talking about a lost pair of socks."

Harlan scowled. "The furniture thing is just a hobby."

Tobias sighed. "There's nothing wrong with following your dreams, Harlan."

Harlan picked up the pen again. "I'm living my dream, Tobias. I don't need another one."

Sophie was surrounded by people in love. And all it was doing was making her grumpy.

Kevin had been planted on one of the shop's bar stools

for the better part of two hours, while Lulu tended the coffee pots and steamer. "I think you're the best coffee maker in the state," Kevin said, as Lulu handed him his third cup of the day. "Never tasted anything quite as great as the cups you brew, Lulu."

"Then you need to expand your horizons," Lulu said, but her words lacked bite and a slight smile curved across her face. "Or get new taste buds."

Kevin sent Lulu a wink. "I think it's because I'm being served by the prettiest barista in Florida."

Lulu flicked a dishtowel at him. "All the sweet talking in the world isn't going to get you a free refill, you old goat."

Across the way, Mildred and Art were cozied up together on the same side of a booth, sharing a platter of cookies and a hot pot of tea. Even three days into the Love Lottery, they were giggling like a couple of teenagers. Two other couples were snuggling in the shop, more evidence of Mildred's matchmaking abilities.

Too bad she'd made such a huge blunder in pairing Sophie and Harlan. Maybe her matchmaking instincts were all burned out by the time she got to that match.

It wasn't that Harlan Jones wasn't handsome. He was. It wasn't that his voice didn't turn on some switch deep inside her. It did.

It wasn't that he hadn't intrigued her. She'd seen two different sides of Harlan—the public radio personality and the man who had helped her grandmother home and not left until Grandma had drank an entire glass of iced tea and had put her feet up. And then there was the man who had resisted when she'd said he should make a business out of his furniture building—he was hiding the reason why behind those blue eyes. And a part of her really wanted to know what that was.

A crazy part. Hadn't she been fooled by charm and fame before? Not again.

Sophie propped her chin in her hands, and watched the foot traffic go by outside the shop. She'd hung up a sign announcing Cuppa Java Café as the official headquarters of the Love Lottery, but so far, even with the promo on the radio yesterday morning, it hadn't seemed to make a dent in business. What she needed was what Harlan had suggested—damn him for being right—some kind of event, one that would get people talking and noticing Cuppa Java Café.

A crowd of college students burst into the shop. "Yeah, I think this is the place," a tall, skinny boy in glasses said. "Quick, let's get a table before he gets here."

Before he gets here? Sophie wondered about that, then remembered she had a musician scheduled for tonight. Goodness, his fans must be loyal to be here this early.

The group commandeered a quartet of tables, dragging them across the floor to form one big seating arrangement. There was a flurry of chair moving, and people moving, before they all settled down. Sophie flipped out an order pad and crossed to the group. "Hi, everyone. Welcome to Cuppa Java Cafe. What can I get you?"

The tall boy leaned forward on his elbows. "Do you know what time he's getting here?"

"The guitarist for tonight?" Sophie flicked out her watch. "About seven. He'll play two sets—"

"No, not him. The Love Doctor." As soon as the words left the boy's mouth, the girls around him began to giggle. The boy's face reddened. "Well, that's what he calls himself."

"Yeah, you need a doctor, Charlie," said one of the other boys. "A head doctor."

"Is he coming?" one of the girls asked. "Because Harlan

said they'd be doing a special live feed right here. And they'd have guests come on, to ask the Love Doctor relationship questions."

"Harlan said what?" Fury rose in Sophie at the gall of Harlan Jones to think he could just march in here, with that Love Doctor guy, and broadcast a live radio show without even asking her first. The nerve of that man!

Then, as she turned the idea over in her mind, she realized it could work. Maybe even be the answer she wanted. Maybe with this event, she could garner the publicity she'd been looking for. Finally put her little shop square on the map of must-see destinations in the Tampa Bay area.

Harlan Jones had suddenly turned into her best ally. And he didn't even know it.

Yet.

"She's going to kill me."

Ernie clapped Harlan on the shoulder. "Quite the contrary, my friend. What better way to show a woman you're interested than by making a public declaration?"

"But I'm not interested, Ernie. I—"

"Tell yourself that all you want," Ernie said with a laugh. "I've seen the way you look at her. Like a coyote watching a lone little sheep that got cut away from the flock."

Harlan chuckled. "Did anyone ever tell you that your metaphors are horrible?"

"Doesn't matter, long as they're right."

"Harlan, we're live in ten," Carl, the remote tech, said. "And we still have to get the mikes and everything set up."

"Let me clear it with the owner." Harlan headed inside the coffee shop, prepared to do battle with Sophie Watson. If he could get a word in edgewise, then maybe he could make her see this live feed was a great idea. He braced himself, then entered the coffee shop.

"Hello, Mr. Jones," Sophie said. She greeted him with a smile, and a freshly brewed cup of Earl Grey. "Do you or your crew need anything? Might be good to get something to drink before you start the show."

He'd had an argument waiting on the tip of his tongue. But Sophie had gone and turned the tables on him, and he stood there, as mute as a scarecrow. "Uh…thank you."

She smiled. "My pleasure."

The way those two words curled off her tongue made his insides go hot and liquid. He wasn't used to being surprised by a woman, or feeling off-kilter around any female, but this Sophie Watson—

She kept him teetering on his toes.

What had happened? Was she just trying to trick him? Because last he checked, she'd been madder than a wet hen, and ready to drag him and his dogs into court. But here she was, smiling at him as if they were the friendliest of neighbors.

Hmm. He didn't like that. At all.

He thumbed toward the front of the shop. "We're just going to set up—"

"Out front, in your chairs? I think that's a terrific idea. If it gets too hot out there, feel free to come inside."

She was finishing his sentences now, too? What the hell? And why was she suddenly so agreeable? It had to be more than just the little bit of promo he'd given the Love Lottery and the community wellness center on his show. And much more than him pouring a glass of iced tea for her grandmother.

His gaze narrowed. "What's got you being so co-operative?"

"I've seen the advantages in working with you instead of

against you." She patted his chest. A simple touch, nothing more than a brush, really, but it sent his mind down some decidedly complicated paths. Ones that the two of them had come dangerously close to treading already. "Consider me your newest ally, Harlan Jones."

He captured her hand in his and her eyes widened in surprise. Her mouth dropped into a little O. Damn. Why hadn't he kissed her the other day? Desire raged inside him.

"That could be dangerous," he said, his voice low and dark.

"I like danger," she said, then slipped out of his grasp and walked away.

He grinned. Hot damn. That woman was a contradiction in a hundred different ways. He imagined himself exploring each and every one of them, starting with that sassy mouth, then trailing his lips down her throat, along the curve of her breasts—

"Harlan, we're all set." Carl's voice interrupted Harlan's fantasy.

"Great. Time to get to work." He said the words more to remind himself than Carl. For a second, there he'd gone off the trail. He needed to stick to the plan—a plan that didn't include a relationship with Sophie Watson.

Harlan settled in one of the two chairs he had made, while Ernie plopped into the other. Carl fitted the two men with headsets, then adjusted their microphones. Then he stepped back and, with his fingers, began counting down to airtime.

When Carl gave the "go" signal, Harlan started speaking. "Welcome to *Horsin' Around with Harlan*. Yep, folks, that's right, a bonus show in the middle of the day, being broadcast live from Cuppa Java Café, right in downtown Edgerton Shores. And all you listeners out there who have computer access, today is the day that WFFM launches its live webstream. Tell your friends, tell your family, because anyone, anywhere can now listen to *Horsin' Around with Harlan*." It had taken a case of beer and a lot of cajoling to get the tech guy to stay late yesterday and implement the webstream, but Harlan was sure this would be the ticket to expanding the station's reach—and in turn netting bigger guests, and bigger ad dollars. "Today, I've got a special guest with me. Ernie Watson, the Love Doctor." He drew out the last two words, giving them a seductive spin. "He's here to answer all your questions about finding that special person. Welcome to the show, Ernie."

"Thanks for having me, Harlan," Ernie said. Beside him, people lined up by a third mike, waiting to ask Ernie questions. "I have to say, I like Edgerton Shores."

"Really? Why?" They'd practiced a little of this banter earlier today, putting together a nice setup for the questions on dating.

"Because it's so filled with *love,*" he emphasized the last word. "Why, that town-wide Love Lottery has got people's hearts all aflutter."

Harlan laughed. "Maybe we need to host a wedding lottery after this."

"Indeed," Ernie said. "If we can get Edgerton Shores' most eligible bachelor hitched, hell, that would be national news."

Harlan sent Ernie a warning glare. The one thing he had told Ernie was off-limits was Harlan's love life.

He'd promised Sophie. First step in keeping that promise—not talk about her. "How about we take some questions?" Harlan said, changing the subject. "I know there are a few people who've been waiting to ask you for advice."

The first question came from a college student who

was suffering from unrequited love. Ernie told him that if he moved on, he might have better luck. "Harlan, what do you think?"

"Sometimes," Harlan added, "the grass looks a lot greener when it moves to another pasture."

"And sometimes," Ernie said, "what you got in your own pasture is perfect." Ernie waved toward the coffee shop, indicating Sophie Watson.

Harlan scowled at Ernie. Damn, the man was stubborn. He'd been friends with Ernie for years. Surely he, of all people, would understand why Harlan had put dating on the back burner for now.

Three more college students asked questions that ranged from the best time to propose to dealing with parents who were less than enthusiastic about a couple being together. Ernie answered them all with a dose of wisdom and a dollop of his sarcastic humor, calling on Harlan from time to time to add his two cents, too.

"We'll be right back," Harlan said when Ernie finished the last question, "after we hear these messages from our sponsors."

"And when we return, we'll put Harlan on the spot about his love life," Ernie blurted into the mike, just before an advertisement cut him off.

"What the hell was that?" Harlan asked, as the ad played in his ear, telling him his mike was off for now. "The deal was we talk just to the townspeople."

"Don't you live in this town, too?" Ernie arched a brow. "Come on, Harlan. Your audience wants to hear your love story."

He'd been giving them more details than he cared to about his relationship with Sophie. Lately, though, he'd wanted to keep more of that private. Close the door to his listening public. "I told you, we're not talking about that."

Sophie slipped around in front of them, exchanging Harlan's now cold tea for a fresh mug. Had she heard that exchange? If so, it didn't show in her features, which were as placid as a lake at twilight. "The show seems to be going great. I've got three dozen people inside, ordering lattes while they wait to ask their questions. It's exactly the kind of boost my business needed. Thank you."

Gratitude shone in her eyes. When she'd asked him to help her create more publicity for her shop, he'd seen it then as an opportunity to get what he wanted—more attention for the radio station. He'd concocted this live show stunt, not for her, but for WFFM, all under the guise of doing what she'd asked—giving the shop a little PR.

But as he saw the unspoken thank-you on her face, he found himself experiencing a new feeling.

Sympathy.

He understood, after his weeks at the helm of his brother's radio station, just how much pressure lay on the shoulders of a business owner, particularly one struggling to be noticed in a crowded marketplace. Had he been so focused on Tobias and improving Tobias's bottom line that he had missed the impact on those around him?

All those jokes. All that "harmless fun," as he'd called it, had been hurting her. Damn.

Harlan cleared his throat, and held up the hot mug. "Thanks."

She smiled. "No problem."

The urge to say more, to tell her he understood, rose in his chest. Before he could speak, the commercial break was over. The music for the last ad faded away. Harlan held up a finger to Sophie, asking her to wait—they only had a few minutes before they broke again for the news. Maybe he could slip in something more about her shop.

"Welcome back to *Horsin' Around with Harlan*," he said. "We're live outside the Cuppa Java Café in downtown Edgerton Shores. If you want a cup of coffee that'll keep you running the rodeo—" at that, he glanced at Sophie and she flashed him a smile that warmed him through and through "—then this is the place to come. Right now, we've got a whole line of people wanting to talk to Ernie Watson, the Love Doctor. Let's take another question."

As Harlan said that, a skinny boy in his early twenties stood up to the mike, gripping it like it was a lifeline. He licked his lips several times, and shifted from foot to foot.

"Before we take our next question," Ernie cut in, "I say we turn the tables. And ask Miss Sophie here a few questions."

Harlan cursed the live feed. He couldn't say anything without sounding like a jerk. He had to go with the flow, make it sound like it was all part of the show. "Sounds like a great idea, Ernie." Harlan turned to Sophie, and hoped her good mood would extend to being part of the show. After all, this could be the promo she needed—if he kept it all positive. "Sophie, why don't you join us?"

She started to sputter a protest, her eyes wide. The college student at the mike jerked the stand away, clearly not about to give up his place in line. "I've, uh, got coffees to make," she said.

"Come on, now. It'll be great to hear the owner of Cuppa Java Café's take on this whole Love Lottery thing, don't you think?" He gave her an encouraging grin, but still she hesitated.

"Folks, let's encourage our shy Sophie here," Ernie

said, gesturing toward the crowd gathered on the sidewalk. "Sophie, Sophie!"

The other people joined in, until Sophie's name carried on a wave of voices. Her eyes widened even more, and she looked ready to bolt. Harlan should have let her go, should have moved on to the skinny boy's question, but her reluctance intrigued him. Didn't she trust him, after the morning at the station?

Well, considering that had been followed by Ernie's arrival, maybe she didn't. He'd have to change that. Before he could think twice, he reached out and tugged her over to him. He tugged a little too hard, though, and instead of Sophie stopping at his side, she tumbled into his lap.

He caught a whiff of her perfume—something with vanilla and jasmine, the fragrance notes low and smoky. Her skin brushed against his, warm, smooth, intoxicating.

If looks could kill, Sophie would have severed an artery with her gaze. She scrambled out of Harlan's lap. She brushed at her skirt, as if wiping every trace of him off the cotton fabric. "You have a way of making a point, Mr. Jones."

Ernie chuckled. "Seems you two don't need a prescription from the Love Doctor. You're mixing up your own formula right here on live radio."

"The only thing getting mixed here is caramel frappuccinos," Sophie said. The crowd behind her laughed.

"And why is that?" Ernie asked, leaning in toward Sophie. "Seems to me, we have two lonely hearts here, just made for each other."

"I'm not interested in a relationship," Sophie said. Her gaze darted to the side, clearly looking for an escape route. "And I don't want to talk about my love life on the radio."

"Why not?" Ernie asked.

"I'm busy."

Ernie waved a hand in a wide arc. That was Ernie—every movement and gesture was exaggerated and larger than life. "You're never too busy for love," he said. "Because if love's going to find you, it's going to do it on its timetable, not yours."

Sophie shook her head. "I don't think—"

"Take this Love Lottery. I bet you were just as busy before your name was paired up with Harlan's here, as you were after."

"Well, yes, but—"

"So love just plopped itself right into your lap. Sort of the same way you just plopped into Harlan's a second ago." Ernie chuckled.

Harlan knew he should get this derailed train back on the tracks, but truth be told, he was as interested in Sophie's answers as Ernie. Why was she so resistant to dating? Was it him? Or men in general?

"I think," Ernie said, rising out of his chair and taking the microphone with him as he crossed to Sophie, "that you need to grab love by the horns and hold on for the ride."

"And I think I need to get back inside and finish making the coffee before the customers riot." She still had that wide-eyed nervous look about her. Being in the spotlight wasn't a place she liked to be.

It didn't make sense to Harlan. If she played it right, she could get publicity for her shop. She seemed determined to avoid being in the public eye.

"I say the two of you should kiss," Ernie said. "Then you'll see what prize the Love Lottery has brought you!"

Now he'd gone too far. Love Doctor or no Love Doctor, this was too much. Harlan got to his feet, forgetting about the mike beside him, the listeners who were eating up every word. "Ernie, I think—"

But Harlan's objections were drowned out by the crowd, which had hopped on Ernie's bandwagon with enthusiasm. "Kiss! Kiss! Kiss!" they shouted, then the crowd pressed in closer, enveloping them in a crush of people.

Sophie had that deer-in-the-headlights look, and Harlan moved toward her, intending to lead her out of the crowd. Ernie must have seen his movements as intention, though, and he clapped Harlan on the back. "Give her a kiss she'll remember, Harlan, my boy," Ernie said. "Show people what winners get in the Love Lottery."

"Kiss! Kiss! Kiss!" the crowd chanted. The sound rose in volume until it seemed to echo off the surrounding buildings.

As the crowd pressed forward, the distance between Sophie and him narrowed until she was mere inches away. He inhaled, catching the sweet, sexy notes of her perfume. Desire coiled inside him, tightening with every millimeter of winnowing distance between them, until he could think of nothing but holding her, touching her, kissing her. He'd wanted to kiss her, almost from the first moment they'd met.

"Seems the crowd wants a kiss," he said.

"I don't care what the crowd wants." She raised her chin, a defiant, stormy look on her face. He should have backed away.

He didn't.

"Kiss! Kiss! Kiss!"

He reached up and traced along her jaw. "What do you want, Sophie?"

"I want…" Her voice trailed off and her gaze dropped to his lips. The crowd dropped away, and it was just them.

And the kiss they both had been waiting for. One they had danced around so many times. "Harlan."

Hearing his name was all he needed. He reached up, cupped her jaw with both hands, then brought his mouth to hers, hovering above her lips for one long, sweet second. Anticipation filled him, and he became intently aware of how she felt beneath him, how lush her lips looked.

The chants of the crowd became a distant din. All he saw, all he noticed, was Sophie's breath whispering in and out between her slightly parted lips, and the dark ocean filling her green eyes.

He lowered his head, and captured her mouth, soft and slow at first, just a sweet, sweet taste. She didn't respond for a moment, then in tiny degrees she went soft against him, her mouth opening to his, her body yielding to his touch. His fingers inched along the tender skin of her jaw, capturing more of her, drawing her closer.

She tasted like candy, like a luscious dessert he had never sampled before. He'd expected sassy, spicy even, but Sophie Watson's kiss was tender, delightful. Unforgettable.

The piercing sound of wolf whistles cut through the fog in Harlan's brain, and he stepped back, releasing Sophie. Her lips were flush from their kiss, and a soft pink had risen in her cheeks. When his gaze met hers, she glanced away.

So. He wasn't the only one affected by that kiss.

Ernie clapped him hard on the back again. "Now that's what I'm talking about! That's love right there, folks. True love."

"No," Sophie said. "That was a mistake. One I won't be repeating." She shoved her way through the crowd and disappeared inside the shop.

CHAPTER SEVEN

SOPHIE snuck out the back door before Harlan ended his show. Lulu called her a coward, but she told herself it was self-preservation. She'd gone home to work on the shop's books, and spent the afternoon essentially avoiding Harlan.

What had she been thinking? Kissing Harlan Jones, of all people, and doing it right there, in the middle of the sidewalk while half the town cheered her on? In front of her shop at that? She'd been in some kind of fog, that was for sure, or maybe she'd just caved to the peer pressure of a dozen chanting people.

But it hadn't been that, and she knew it. She'd wanted him to kiss her.

She'd wanted him to kiss her for days now. Had thought about almost nothing else since that near-kiss at the radio station. And when he'd zeroed in on her, and asked her what she'd wanted, she'd thought only of one thing.

Him.

And now she'd gone and done the one thing she didn't want to do—create yet another public spectacle. Lord, the gossip would be flying fast and furious after this. Undoubtedly, the newspapers would carry the story, one after another like dominoes. Maybe she could just hide in her house for like the next century.

"Hello? Sophie?" Mildred's voice carried through the front door. "Are you home?"

"Of course she is, Mildred," Grandma Watson said. "Her front door is wide-open."

"Maybe there's a robber inside. Hang on a minute, let me get my pepper spray."

Sophie heard the clanging of things in Mildred's massive purse, and bit back a laugh. "I'm in the kitchen," she called out, then poked her head around the corner just to be sure they'd heard her. "No need to pepper spray me."

Mildred muttered a curse and tucked the can back in her purse. "One of these days, I'm going to need this thing."

Sophie invited her grandmother and Mildred into the kitchen, and made a pitcher of raspberry iced tea. The afternoon sun was high in the sky outside, and the women were parched. She poured them each a glass, and set them on the table. Maybe their company would help take her mind off that disaster with Harlan Jones. She could just imagine what he'd be saying about her on his radio show tomorrow.

No, she definitely didn't want to imagine that. Oh, why had she kissed him?

"What, no cookies?" Grandma said. And pouted. Actually pouted.

Sophie laughed, then retrieved a box from the breadbox. "Here you are. Chocolate chip."

Grandma and Mildred each took a cookie, then gestured to Sophie to join them. "So," Mildred said, leaning in close, "I hear you kissed Harlan Jones today."

"It was on the radio and everything," Grandma said. "And I heard that reporter from the *Edgerton Shores Weekly* is going to do a little piece in his About Town column on it."

"Just what I need. Bet the wire services can't wait to

run with that one." Sophie groaned. Kissing Harlan had been the biggest mistake she could make, yet every ounce of her wanted to do it again.

Damn that man.

"I'm sure the news isn't going to pick up that story," Mildred said. "Why, it's not nearly as big as running out on a senate candidate."

"Gee, thanks."

Grandma laughed. "It'll be fine. It always is."

Sophie toyed with a cookie. "I just don't want people thinking of me as that woman who ran out on her wedding. Or the woman who kissed Harlan Jones on live radio. I want people to see me as a serious businesswoman."

"And where's the fun in that?" Mildred said. "You can have fun and run a business. Why, you've been doing exactly that this past week."

Sophie let out a gust of frustration, then turned away to refill her glass, even though it was still half full. "I've got to get back to work."

"No, you don't," Mildred said, getting to her feet and grabbing her purse. "It's already after four. You have a carnival to get to."

Sophie groaned. She'd completely forgotten about tonight's Spring Fling activity. Yet another sign that Harlan Jones was all wrong for her. One kiss and her brain emptied like a dam with a hole.

Mildred and Grandma left, taking extra cookies with them just in case. Sophie returned to her paperwork. Maybe if she went late to the carnival she could avoid—

Her doorbell rang. Sophie turned down the hall, and froze.

Harlan Jones's dogs were peeking in her front windows, one on either side of the door, tongues lolling and leaving streaks of saliva on the glass. She doubted the dogs could ring the doorbell, so that meant if the canine terrors were here, so was Harlan Jones.

"Let me guess," she said as she opened the door. "I left the show and so you dragged it all the way to my house."

The edges of his smile were shadowed by the brim of his hat. "Not at all. I'm here for honorable reasons."

"What honorable reasons do you have for anything?"

"I've come calling, Miss Watson. I do believe we have a date at the carnival."

"I don't think it's a good idea if we go together."

"Well, I do." He crooked his arm toward her. "Shall we?"

Just when she thought she'd rid herself of Harlan Jones, he popped back up like a bad penny. "Listen, you don't have to go through with these dates. I'm sure there are plenty of couples who aren't working out, and stopped participating."

"Who says we aren't working out?"

"I'd think that's obvious. We barely get along."

He took a step closer. The temperature of the air quadrupled. "I'm afraid I have to disagree." His voice dropped to a low, rough whisper. "Didn't you enjoy that kiss?"

Just the mention of it sent a bolt of heat through her veins. She forced herself to hold her ground, not to betray the urge to arch her back and lean into him, and offer her lips to his again. One kiss didn't make for a relationship. Especially not one that Harlan had used as entertainment for his listeners.

Just when she thought she knew him, he proved her wrong.

"That was merely a publicity stunt," she said. "For your show."

"No, sugar, it was anything but."

"Are you really going to stand there and tell me that kissing me on *live radio* wasn't about boosting your ratings?"

"It wasn't." He moved a little closer and his hat's shadow dropped over her. "Let me show you."

"Show me?"

He nodded. Slow. Once. "Show you that kiss was real. That I was as knocked off my boots as you."

She shook her head. "I don't believe that for a second."

"Then let me prove it to you, darlin'." Before she could react, he cupped the back of her head and drew her mouth to his. There was no soft lead-in with this kiss. It was hard and fast and hot. Her pulse jumped into overdrive, and heat flooded her body. His tongue swept into her mouth, teased along hers. Desire exploded in her brain, and she pressed into him, opening her mouth wider, wanting more, wanting...

Just wanting.

He deepened the kiss, his fingers tangling in her hair, his other hand coming around to splay against her back, fingertips dancing below the waistband of her skirt. He played against her mouth, his lips creating a deep, dark melody that whispered promises of a crescendo she would never forget.

God, he was good. He tasted like coffee and smelled like soap and hard work. The brim of his hat brushed against her hair, as if every part of him wanted to touch her. She stopped thinking, stopped doing anything but returning his kiss, her body pressing into his, asking without saying for more. For everything.

She'd never been kissed quite like this, and had never wanted a kiss to last forever as much as she did this one.

But Harlan drew back, his fingers slowly untangling

from her hair, drifting along her neck for a brief second before his touch left her. "*That,* darlin', was no publicity stunt."

What the hell was he thinking?

Well, he hadn't been. That was as sure as rain in spring. A half hour had passed since Harlan had kissed Sophie on her porch. And ever since, he'd been unable to think of anything but kissing her again. He should have been concentrating on manning the radio station's booth at the carnival. Should have had his mind on joking with Ernie, and making the most out of this opportunity with the listeners. But his attention was divided, with the lion's share of it locked on Sophie Watson.

They had hurried over to the carnival, getting there with seconds to spare before Sophie needed to make the announcement opening it to the public. She'd been nervous on stage, a much more stressed woman than the one who ran the coffee shop.

Because of that kiss? Or because she was overworked and unhappy about having him tag along?

He told himself he didn't need to know. But that was a lie.

The show ended, and Harlan glanced over at Sophie. "Go ahead," Carl said, seeing Harlan's interest. "We can get this."

Harlan hesitated, then headed toward her. Maybe if he spent some more time with her, he'd remember why she annoyed him so much. Because damned if he could quite recall right now.

Sophie was standing beside the Tilt-A-Whirl, watching people spin around while pop music played in the background. She was wearing a white lace-trimmed sundress today, with flat shoes. She'd left her hair down, and done something that made it curl around her shoulders. The outfit made her look as sweet and fresh as the spring air. He slipped in beside her. "Want to try it out?"

She jumped at the sound of his voice, and before she could stop it, a smile curved across her face. When she smiled, it was as if the early evening sunlight had kissed her features. For a second, looking at Sophie made Harlan wonder if his all-work philosophy had him missing out on something that could be incredible.

"I really should be working the ticket booth," she said. "Mildred said we're shorthanded."

The ride came to a stop and people began disembarking. From the corner of his eye, Harlan saw his brother head over to the station's booth. Tobias's movements were jerky and stuttered because of the crutches and cast. Harlan should head over to the booth, and make sure his brother went home. Tobias needed to rest, not worry about WFFM.

Guilt warred with desire. Harlan took Sophie's hand in his. Her palm was soft and delicate against his big, beefy paw. Surely he had five minutes, too, to take a spin. Just five minutes, that was all. And for that snippet of time, maybe he could taste what he'd been missing.

"Why, Miss Sophie," he said, "how can you sell the rodeo if you haven't taken the bronco for a spin?"

"I…" She glanced again at the ride. The operator was waving in the next group. Her gaze went to the ticket booth, then back to the laughing, happy people climbing into the Tilt-A-Whirl's cars. "Okay. Just one ride."

As he followed Sophie through the gate and handed their tickets to the ride operator, he told himself he wasn't just doing this for himself, he was doing this for the show, for the radio station, and ultimately, for his brother. So he'd have an adventure to recount tomorrow. After all, he'd agreed to this Love Lottery thing. Might as well make the most of it.

But as he slid in beside Sophie into the cove-shaped car and pulled the bar over their laps, he knew he was lying to himself. He wanted to feel her body slide against his when the ride spun around a curve. He wanted to hear her laugh and see her smile, and know that he had been a part of that. He wanted to be with her, even if it was only for a couple of minutes. He didn't want to think about work, not while he was here with her. And especially not while she was smiling.

For the hundredth time that day, he asked himself what the hell he was doing. He had a business to run, a brother to worry about, a radio show to host. He didn't have time for a woman like Sophie Watson. She had small-town, settle-down, make-a-family written all over her.

He sure as hell wasn't here to settle down or make a family. He shouldn't even entertain the notion. People depended on him to stay on task—not get distracted by a woman.

Tinny pop music played inside the car. A warm breeze whispered the scent of the ocean. Beside him, he noticed Sophie tense. Her fingers wrapped around the thick metal bar.

"What's the matter? The ride make you nervous?"

"No. I just—" she sighed "—saw a reporter over there. I'm hoping he's not here to talk to me."

"I thought you were publicity director for the Love Lottery thing. Doesn't that include talking to the media?" Everything he knew about this woman spoke of confidence, strength. She didn't seem the type to back down from a challenge, or heck, even two golden retrievers. Why did talking to the press or making a short speech get her so worked up?

She didn't answer his question. "How do you do your show and share your life with your listeners, and not wind up nervous that you might say too much?"

"I don't really think about it," he said. "I just…talk."

"Aren't you worried you'll say or do something that will embarrass you?"

Harlan laughed. "Darlin', I have made a career out of my embarrassin' moments." Except lately he'd begun to wonder if maybe being so open was a mistake. Thousands of people thought they knew him when really, no one did. No one knew the Harlan Jones that existed outside that radio booth.

His gaze took in Sophie's delicate features, her earnest expression. At that moment, he could see she was genuinely interested in him and his thoughts. Him—Harlan Jones the man, not the personality. The same man who'd grown up poor in a tiny house in Dallas.

Right now, there was no tension between them. Merely a conversation between…well, friends. And it was nice, nicer than he'd expected.

"Doesn't that ever get to you? Having people know every detail of your private life?" she asked, as if she'd read his mind.

He considered putting his radio face on his answer. Telling her he was just fine with it, that it was all part of the show. Instead, he did what he'd never done before—

And gave Sophie Watson a peek at the truth.

"Yeah," he said, "it does. People think they know me when really, they only know the person I've painted for them, if that makes sense."

"It does," she said softly, and once again, he wondered if there was something she was holding back. She seemed to understand, in a way few people he knew did. "Then why do you keep doing the show?"

"In the beginning, it was fun. I'm not gonna lie to you, darlin', it's mighty nice to get recognized on the street, to have people ask you to dinner, just because you're some kind of celebrity."

"Or have a certain level of notoriety."

"I do indeed," he said, laughing.

"But?" she prompted. "I can hear a but in your sentence."

"But after a while, I started to wonder…" His voice trailed off. Damn. This sharing thing was hard. No wonder he'd avoided doing it most of his life.

"Go ahead, finish what you were saying."

He took off his hat and spun it between his fingers. "But after a while, I started to wonder if people liked the Harlan they thought they knew, the radio version, or, well, hell, the real me."

"The real you isn't so bad," she said, and a smile curved across her face.

"Why, thank you, ma'am. And neither is the real Sophie."

Her gaze went to some far off place. "I understand what you mean, though. People see or hear about what happens in public, and that becomes their frame for your picture. They don't bother to dig any deeper."

The tension had returned to her shoulders, to her jaw. "Sounds like you've had an embarrassing moment you'd like to take back," he said.

She shrugged. "Maybe."

He peered around her face and looked at her until she turned her green eyes on his. Whatever had happened, she wasn't betraying a word. "And you don't want to tell me because you're afraid I'll put it on the show."

"Wouldn't you? You've put everything else I've ever done on your show."

Ouch. The truth stung, and regret pinged Harlan. If he

could take the words back, he would. Because he hated seeing that disappointed, hurt look on Sophie's face, and he hated even more knowing that he put it there. "I have, but I haven't made you look bad."

"'Animal antagonist'?"

"Okay, maybe with that."

"'Lunatic neighbor'?"

He cringed. "Yeah, that, too."

"Shall I go on?"

The ride operator had finished making sure everyone was safe in the cars and was crossing the platform, his steps making their seat bounce a little. In a minute, the ride would start. It would sure be a waste to embark on a fun event like this, with Sophie steaming at him.

"I'm sorry," Harlan said, and honestly meant the words. "That was wrong of me. Sometimes I need to lasso my mouth before it gets away from my brain."

He could see her try to hold back a smile at his lame attempt at a joke, but the effort was too much, and she gave up. The smile swung across her face, wide and bright, and it seemed as if the sun had suddenly risen inside the shadows of the cove-shaped ride. He hadn't realized how much he wanted her to forgive him until she did.

"Does that mean you aren't going to say anything mean about me ever again?" she asked.

He made a gesture of crossing his heart. "Nothing mean. I promise."

She snorted. But the smile stayed. "I'll believe that when I hear it."

He grinned. "I thought you didn't listen to my show."

"I don't."

"Then how will you ever know what I say about you?"

"The ride's starting. We should pay attention." And she

looked away from him so he couldn't tell what she might have said, if she'd answered his question.

This woman drove him crazy. Half the time he was thinking about kissing her, the other half he thought about getting as far away as possible. Right this second, he wanted nothing more than to see her smile again. And to find out what mysteries she was keeping to herself.

For the first time in a long time, Harlan Jones thought about sharing his own mysteries with another person. Gettin' real, as they called it, and letting Sophie Watson in.

He considered her again. It took him a second to make the connection, to start bringing all the pieces from the last few days together. "Is all this because of what happened during the live radio show earlier? I'm real sorry about that. Things just kind of got out of hand."

She worried her bottom lip. "It happened. Nothing I can do about it but move forward."

"Actually," he said as the ride started, "I think right now we're gonna move in circles." The car began spinning slowly at first, then picking up speed as the platform spun faster. The world outside went from details—Ernie waiting by the radio station's booth, Tobias sitting on a stool beside him, Mildred and Art walking hand in hand—to a blur of colors. The bright red car began to sway in half circles back and forth, and Sophie gripped the silver bar to keep from sliding. But as it moved faster, centrifugal force spun the car in a full, fast circle, peeling her away from the bar, and into his chest.

She was solid and warm against him, and with each spin he caught the vanilla notes of her perfume. How did that woman manage to smell so…delicious? It was as if she'd taken the sweetest ingredients in those bis-yummy things and applied them to her skin. He wanted to taste her skin, trail his mouth along her shoulders, her arms, her belly, and see if she tasted as wonderful as she smelled. Desire pulsed in his veins, thundered in his head.

Kiss her, kiss her.

His brain chanted the words, just like the crowd had earlier. *Kiss her, kiss her.* Instead, he raised his arm above her shoulders and she curved into him on the next turn, as if she'd been made for that space.

"Oh, sorry," she said. She reached for the bar again, and tried to pull herself off him but the ride's movements kept her rooted in place. The wind toyed with her hair, sending the blond strands up and away from her face like a delicate halo.

"You're fine, totally fine," Harlan said. "This is probably as close as I'll come to rescuing a damsel in distress."

She laughed, a sweet, hearty sound that was music to Harlan's ears. "It's moving so fast!"

"Yeah, it is," he said. Faster than he wanted, but he couldn't seem to put on the brakes. They spun in quick, tight circles, Sophie pressed hard against him, and Harlan's mind traveled down paths that went way beyond trailing kisses down her body. He wondered what it would be like to have her in his arms every day. To come home to her smiling face, and even more, to wake up to her curled against him. Every time the car made another loop, he fought the urge to do more than just hold her.

He hadn't felt this much desire for a woman in…well, forever. Harlan Jones was a man who worked hard, who put everything he had into the job he was doing. He wasn't a man who gave in to fancy flights of reason. And everything about being involved with Sophie Watson would be like riding a jet plane away from the reality of his days, his job. What his brother needed from him.

Didn't make him stop wanting her, though.

"Are you having fun?" she asked.

"Yep," he said, and his words were caught in the vortex inside the car. "Are you?"

She nodded. "Lots."

"Good," Harlan murmured against her neck. The word was lost in the golden maze of her hair. And so was he.

Too soon, the ride came to an end. The car began to slow, and Sophie shifted away from him. Disappointment sunk in his gut. He wanted her pressed against him again, wanted to feel her one more time in his arms. Wanted to stay in this tiny pocket comprised of just him and her, for a little longer.

The world started coming back into focus, and as the WFFM booth spun in and out of sight, Harlan got back to the real world. His brother waved at him, and even though the early evening sun was still bright, the day was warm, and Tobias hadn't done much more than sit in the station's booth, Harlan could see exhaustion lining his younger brother's face.

Tobias wasn't recovered enough to run the station on his own. Hell, he might never be. That meant Harlan had to keep his eye on the ball, and not go chasing after something that he couldn't have.

Hadn't he already done that once? And that choice had ultimately cost Tobias, nearly cost him everything. Not again.

The ride operator hopped onto the platform, and pulled back the bar. "All done."

"Yeah," Harlan said, following Sophie out of the car, then turning to head toward the station, and his brother. "We are."

CHAPTER EIGHT

MILDRED was wearing a smile that the Cheshire cat would envy when Sophie entered the ticket booth for her shift. Oh, oh, Sophie thought. That didn't bode well.

Sophie had decided on the walk over here that she would tell Mildred to find someone else for Harlan. That would be best for all involved.

Definitely best.

Before the ride started, they'd had a nice conversation, one that made her look at Harlan in a new light. Over the last week, he'd done that a dozen times. In the way he'd taken care of Grandma, the way he'd talked to her—and listened, really listened. The day he had her on his show and focused entirely on what was important to her.

She'd been thinking how nice all that was. How much she enjoyed being with him. Then the ride had started, and the dynamics shifted. In a big way.

Her skin still tingled where he had touched her. She could still feel the imprint of his hard, strong chest against her back, feel the power in his arm when he wrapped it around her. She'd felt safe and protected and…

Desired.

And that was the whole problem. He wanted her, that was clear in his kiss, in his touch. The problem was wanting him back. Because she did. Too much. She had to end this before she got in too much deeper and began thinking about a future with Harlan Jones.

Despite everything he'd said about the drawbacks to his job, he was still a man who wouldn't hesitate to use her most embarrassing moments to entertain the audience. If he found out about what happened in the church, she had no doubt he'd turn that into a joke, just like the rest of the media had. In short, he was dangerous, on a hundred different levels, and that meant she should stay away.

"So," Mildred said. "I see my match is working out."

"I agree. Lulu and Kevin seem very happy," Sophie said.

Mildred laughed and waved a hand. "Silly! I meant you and Harlan."

"Harlan and I? No, no, we're—"

"Happier than two clams in one shell," Mildred said. "Your grandmother is going to be so pleased when she stops by the carnival later."

Mildred's corny phrase immediately sent Sophie's mind back to the Tilt-A-Whirl. Spinning into Harlan's chest, feeling the hard strength of him beneath her. For a second back there, she'd wished he would wrap both his arms around her, trail kisses down her neck, maybe slip a hand beneath the cotton of her T-shirt. Touch her. Make her feel everything she had never felt before. Never felt with Jim, or anyone else.

Then when the ride had slowed, and Harlan had jerked away from her as if that moment of contact was the biggest mistake he'd ever made, she'd come to her senses. She might have seen some nice traits in him lately, but that didn't mean he was settling-down material.

Besides that, she had a Love Lottery to run, a grandmother to worry about and a lot of lattes to make. There was no time to work on anything with Harlan Jones.

Good thing, too, because the man had a way of erasing her self-control.

"Mildred, Harlan and I aren't a couple. Well, we are, but it's just for show, for this week. If I wasn't publicity director, I'd back out." She saw disappointment fill the older woman's features. Sophie's gaze drifted across the park, lingered on the tall man in a cowboy hat leaning against the WFFM booth. He was talking to the other men in the booth, and not looking at her. Thank goodness, because if he did, she wasn't sure she could stick to her resolve. "I know Harlan paid for his match, so why don't you…" She paused, then pushed forward. She had to say it. "Why don't you fix him up with someone else for the rest of the week? That way he gets his money's worth."

And maybe he'd be happier with someone less…complicated, she told herself. Even though the thought of him with another woman sent a sharp pain through her chest.

"Why?"

Sophie jerked her attention back to Mildred. "Why what?"

"Why aren't you and Harlan going to work out?" Mildred's lips puckered and her eyes narrowed. She leaned in closer to Sophie. "Because I've been making matches ever since I married my Henry, God rest his soul, and not a one of the pairs I've put together has broken up."

"None of the couples broke up?"

"Well, if they have, no one's said a word to me. As far as I know, all the chickens are happy in the hen house."

"That's good."

"Darn tootin'," Mildred said. "Why, I've been to more weddings than a priest. So, if you ask me, you should rethink Harlan Jones." Mildred stepped out of the ticket booth, and Sophie turned to the little boy beneath the window.

"Can I help you?"

"Ten tickets, please," he said, and thrust a five-dollar bill at her.

Sophie smiled, and exchanged the money for the tickets. "Have fun!" But her words fell on deaf ears because the boy was already charging across the park, headed for the Ferris wheel.

"I never thought he was right for you, you know," Mildred said.

Sophie turned around, surprised to find Mildred still standing in the doorway. "Who? Harlan? I was just saying that. That's why I think you should find him someone else."

Mildred waved off that suggestion. "No, that Jim fellow. He didn't read right for me."

Mildred had more superstitions than anyone Sophie knew. "Are you doing tarot now, too, Miss Meyers?"

"Goodness, no." She took a step toward Sophie. The ticket booth door shut behind her, and once again, they were enclosed in the tiny space. "Do you want to know how I match people?" Mildred didn't wait for an answer. "I close my eyes, and I imagine two people together. And in my heart, I know if putting those two together will work or not. Jim was a nice man and all, but when I pictured him with you, it never felt right."

"Wish you'd told me before the wedding," Sophie muttered. "Could have saved myself some embarrassment."

"You weren't in any mood for listening. You have one quality, Sophie Watson, that is both good and bad. You are bull-headed."

"I am not." The Smithson family came up to the ticket booth, all three children in tow. The father plunked down a twenty, and Sophie handed him his tickets. The littlest Smithson sent Sophie a little wave before trotting off after her siblings. Her gaze followed him, then stopped when she saw Harlan Jones seated behind the mike in the radio station's booth.

Broadcasting about their conversation in the Tilt-A-Whirl? She sure hoped not. He'd promised. Would he keep his word? How well did she know him, anyway?

"You are indeed bull-headed," Mildred said from behind her. "It's why your coffee shop has succeeded in a place where, heck, half the time, it is too darned hot to drink coffee. It's why you were chosen as the head of the Love Lottery and asked to chair the fundraising committee for the community wellness center, because if anyone could make that happen, it would be you."

Sophie had known Mildred most of her life, and had rarely heard that many compliments in one sitting. Mildred Meyers was a nice, generous and quirky woman, but not one who went throwing about accolades. "Thank you."

Mildred wagged a finger at her. "I also said it could be a bad trait. You are so bull-headed about Harlan Jones that you can't see the truth."

"And what truth is that?" Sophie's gaze strayed to Harlan again. He caught her eye, tipped his hat her way, and something hot exploded in her gut.

"That you two are made for each other. There isn't another woman in the world who's as perfect for that man as you are. So I'm sorry, but my match stays." Mildred gave Sophie a nice, but firm smile. "Just close your eyes, and you'll see what I see. Harlan Jones is the perfect man for you."

If only she was right, Sophie thought with a sigh, then turned away from Harlan and got busy selling tickets.

Night dropped its blanket of blue black light over the Edgerton Shores town park. Families with small children bought one last elephant ear, tossed one last dart at a balloon, took one last spin on the Ferris wheel, then headed home, with tired, happy kids. WFFM switched to its nightly music show, allowing the remote team to dismantle the temporary location and head home.

Harlan stayed after the other guys left. He should get home to the dogs—they'd probably chewed through his living-room sofa by now—but he lingered, letting the twinkling lights in the trees and the soft music streaming from the speakers wash over him. The carnival's sounds and colors were muted a bit, as if with the coming of night, the event strove for a softer touch.

The last couple months, doing Tobias's job and his own, had been hell on wheels, keeping Harlan so busy most days he barely remembered to eat. Even the time he spent sitting in his chairs at Sophie's café were work hours. He made calls, ran numbers, checked emails. He hadn't had too many moments to just…be.

Hell, he didn't have many of those moments ever. Harlan Jones was a man who knew the value of hard work, and stuck to that, day in and day out. Except for the few hours he wasted in the garage woodshop, he kept his nose to the grindstone. But now, the show was over, the crew gone, and though there was a stack of files sitting in Harlan's truck, he let them sit there while he strolled through the carnival.

Sophie Watson was just leaving the ticket booth. She stepped out of the small white structure and brushed her hair off her face, then let out a long breath, as if she, too, was shedding the weight of the day. Shadows dusted the undersides of her eyes, but to Harlan, she looked as beautiful as always.

"Long day?" he called out to her.

She started at the sound of his voice, then relaxed when

she saw who it was. "Yeah. I've been running here and there all week." She sighed. "I seem to have a bad case of volunteeritis."

"Volunteeritis?"

"If someone needs something done, I'm the first to put up my hand." She shook her head. "I'm either too nice or a glutton for punishment."

He closed the gap between them in three strides. Part of him wanted to reach out and capture her hands in his, draw her to him, and take care of her for the rest of the night. There was just something about the carnival's night-time atmosphere that had softened his stance, made him want things he shouldn't have. "I'd go with the too nice option."

"Thanks." She let out another breath, then looked around at the carnival. "I should probably start cleaning up."

"Aren't there other people with volunteeritis who will do that?"

"Yeah, but—"

"Stop right there, darlin'. You look like you haven't eaten all day." He put out his arm. "Let's get something that'll slap some meat on our bones."

She laughed. "I shouldn't."

"You should." He patted his arm. "Come on. I promise not to bite."

As soon as he said the words, a mental image of his mouth, trailing down her soft peach skin, nipping here and there, tasting her sweet body, sprang to his mind. He could almost taste her, almost feel her arching beneath him. He wanted her, more than he could remember wanting anyone. The memory of her kiss—that hot, hard kiss—sprang to his mind. And stayed. Damn.

What was he doing? Why did he keep getting so distracted?

She slipped her hand into his arm, and smiled up at him, completely unaware of the decadent thoughts in Harlan's mind. "Do you like elephant ears?"

"As long as they come with a tall iced tea, I do."

She laughed, and they started walking, navigating around other couples who were playing the games of chance or taking one last spin on a ride. Pop music filled the air, so loud in some places the vibrations from the speakers had the canopies dancing. People cheered when a skinny teenager won a giant dolphin for his girlfriend. She clutched the stuffed animal to her chest and gave her boyfriend a long, barely legal-in-public kiss.

"I love dolphins," Sophie said. "I think they're my favorite animal."

"You want me to win you one?"

"Oh, no. I prefer the real ones. Before I opened the coffee shop, I used to go to the beach every morning to see them. When it's cooler and not so crowded, they like to come in close to shore. They're just amazing." She sighed. "Now I'm so busy in the mornings, I haven't been over to the beach to see them in a while."

"You should go sometime," Harlan said.

"I should." She watched the couple walk away, arm in arm and still kissing. "Sometime."

"I can't remember the last time I went to one of these," Harlan said as they strolled between the carnival games. The lights flashed in a multicolored rainbow, dancing on Sophie's features. "Guess I just got too old."

"You're never too old for a little fun," Sophie said.

"Yeah," Harlan said, glancing over at her, and wondering how she managed to find that balance that had so eluded him for so long, "you're right."

Sophie put a hand on her chest and faked a swoon. "Did I hear you correctly, Mr. Jones? Did you just say I was right?"

He stopped walking, and turned to face her. Her green eyes danced with merriment, and he found a smile curving across his face in answer. He tipped a finger under her chin, his gaze lingering on those full, dark pink lips. "What's it gonna take for you to start calling me by my given name?"

"You want me to call you…" Her lips parted, and a breath whispered out of her, *"Harlan?"*

Desire roared through his veins. He'd heard plenty of people say his name before, but none had had that mixture of sweet and sassy. His hand danced against her jaw, their gazes locked, and the urge to kiss her again—and again and again—surged inside him. "Oh, Sophie."

"Excuse me," a woman said as she brushed past them.

The interruption jarred Harlan back to reality. Hadn't he decided earlier today not to get any more involved with Sophie? That he should concentrate on WFFM, on helping his brother?

His hand dropped away. He stepped back. "I, uh, believe I promised you an elephant ear."

"Oh, yeah. There's a booth, um, over there." Did he hear disappointment in her tone? Or regret? He didn't ask.

They crossed to a squat white trailer, manned by two women wearing bright pink aprons. The scent of cinnamon and butter filled the air around them, so thick, Harlan could nearly taste the dessert on the breeze. "Two elephant ears and two iced teas," Harlan said, handing over some money.

"You don't have to pay for me," Sophie said. She reached

into her pocket, pulled out some bills and handed them to him.

He pressed the money back into her palm. "Of course I do. This is still a date. And when I'm dating a lady, I take care of her. Let me take care of you, Sophie."

Even under the muted lights of the trailer, Harlan could see a pink flush rise in Sophie's cheeks. "Well, thank you."

"Anytime, darlin'." What was he saying? Did he mean taking care of more than just the cost of a snack? For longer than this week? Every time he knew the right thing to focus on, he came right back to focusing on Sophie.

What was wrong with him? A week ago, he'd rather have spent time wrestling a pig than tangling with Sophie Watson. Then they'd shared a couple of dates, a couple of kisses, and one carnival ride, and his mind was traveling down paths that definitely lead down the road of Like. Maybe something more.

No, there'd be no more. Harlan thought of the work waiting in his car, the brother still recovering from an accident, and the people depending on him, and told himself he should leave.

He didn't.

The woman in the trailer handed them their drinks, followed by two steaming fried dough circles. The elephant ears—so named because their large, irregular shape mimicked that of the animal's—glistened with butter, as if begging to be eaten. He inhaled the scent of fried food—the decadent, heavy fragrance that only came with something battered and cooked in a hell of a lot of grease.

"I like mine loaded," Sophie said, crossing to a small table set up with a variety of condiments. "I only get these once a year, at the Spring Fling, and when I do, I go all out."

"You must have mighty strong self-control to resist these all year." Harlan tore off a chunk of warm dough and popped it in his mouth. It melted against his tongue, smooth and rich.

She sprinkled cinnamon sugar on her fried dough, followed by a heaping spoonful of apple slices. Then she forked off a bite and ate it, pausing to smile at the taste before speaking again. "You should see me when we pull a fresh batch of biscotti out of the oven. I have to practically tie myself to the counter to keep from eating them all."

He wagged another piece of dough at her. "Those don't count. As far as I can tell, those bis-yummies don't have a calorie in them."

"Maybe I'll put that on the advertising literature." She laughed again, and Harlan decided he liked the sound so much, he'd do whatever it took to hear it again. They began to walk the fairgrounds, eating their fried dough and admiring the scenery.

"We'd make quite the team," Harlan said, tossing his trash into a bin.

"That could be dangerous. Us working together."

They had reached the end of the carnival area. There were few lights here—only a couple strings of multicolored bulbs looped between the trees. The music had dropped into background noise. They were alone, in a shadowed, quiet area. The kind of place where anything could happen. He took her trash out of her hands, tossed it in the bin. Then rested his hands on her hips and met her gaze. "I like danger. Very much."

"Do you?" A sexy tease lit the notes of her voice, a flirt danced in her eyes.

That was all it took to push Harlan over the edge. "Hell, yes," he said, his voice nearly a growl as he lowered his mouth to hers and did the one thing he'd promised himself he'd never do again.

Kissed Sophie Watson. And kissed her good.

CHAPTER NINE

SOPHIE didn't want the night to end. After that kiss—a fiery, no-holds-barred kiss that would go down in history as one of the top ten kisses in the world—she had found reason after reason to justify staying with Harlan long after the carnival had shut down for the night.

They'd wandered the town park, talking about everything and nothing. She'd heard about his childhood in Texas, how he met Ernie, his first radio job and more about how his loud mouth had landed him on the air. She'd told him about living in the same town all her life, and finding no place else like it in the world, about opening the coffee shop because she believed in supporting the local economy, and about how close she'd grown to her grandma since her parents moved to northern Florida a few years ago.

She could feel them growing closer, feel the threads of a relationship knit between them. It scared her and thrilled her all at once.

Around midnight, they'd headed over to O'Toole's Pub, a small bar on the east end of Main Street. They'd shared a pitcher of beer, a heaping platter of wings, and more conversation. So much, Sophie was sure her voice would be hoarse in the morning. They'd laughed and flirted, and bumped into each other a hundred times, charging the air with sexual tension and desire.

Before they knew it, the clock struck two in the morning and the bar was closing. Sophie should have been tired, but she could hardly think about sleep. Maybe it was all the conversation. Or the simmering attraction between them. Either way, when they hit the sidewalk and turned toward home, she tried not to look disappointed that the night was over.

At the corner, Harlan paused. His blue eyes gleamed in the soft light cast by the globe-shaped lamps lining Main Street. "I have an idea," he said. "Let's go watch the dolphins."

"But it's dark out," Sophie said. "We can't see anything."

He glanced at his watch. "In a few hours, they'll be swimming along the shore. Let's go down to the beach and wait for them."

She laughed. "You're crazy."

"Maybe. Okay, definitely. But I've lived here for almost two months now and haven't set foot on the sand. I lived in Texas forever and rarely got over to the coast."

"Hmm…a fellow workaholic."

"You know what they say about that, don't you?" She shook her head. "All work and no play makes for grumpy ranch hands."

She laughed. "Is that what we are? Ranch hands?"

"Close enough. We both work sunup to sundown, and deal with more crap than we should."

She laughed again. Why had she never noticed before how funny Harlan Jones could be? How enjoyable spending time with him was? The hours had seemed to fly by, and the thought of having even more hours with Harlan filled her with anticipation.

She liked him, genuinely liked him.

"Let's do it," she said, putting her smaller hand into

his large, warm one. All the while thinking she was crazy for doing this, crazy for spending time with a man who could—and probably would—broadcast every detail of her life on the radio. But all she saw right now, all she felt, was Harlan's warmth, his strength, and his touch. "So what will we do between here and sunrise?"

He grinned. "I'm sure we'll think of something."

The innuendo sent a rush of heat through Sophie. Half of her wanted him to suggest spending those hours at his house. The other half was afraid he would—and she would get even more wrapped up in him than she already was. If they took this further than kisses, Sophie knew without a doubt she'd tumble down a rabbit hole she might never escape. Because if his kisses were any indication of his ability to please a woman—

Well, she'd never leave a bed or Harlan again.

"Do you mind if we stop at my house first?" he asked.

Oh, God, he'd said it. Stop at his house. Take the next step.

She could say no right now and head home. It was the wisest choice, really. The one that kept her far from all temptation.

"I have to let the dogs out," he said when she hesitated, and Sophie felt silly for even thinking he'd meant anything else.

She thought back to those amazing, one-of-a-kind, earth-shattering kisses. Had that been a fluke? Or did he want more?

More that that, did *she* want more? All the way back to his house, she tried to decide. And couldn't. Instead, she opted to part ways when they reached his house, telling him she wanted to run home and change into something warmer since the temperature had dropped during the night. She took the time to pack them a picnic breakfast, and grab a thick blanket to use on the beach. By the time she met up with Harlan again, it was after four. He was waiting in his truck in her driveway, a clear sign that he hadn't intended to take her back to his house and up to his bedroom.

A part of her was relieved. Another part was very disappointed.

"We're crazy," she said after she climbed inside his truck. He had the dogs in the back—something she wasn't thrilled about—so she kept the cooler and the blanket up front with her. Knowing Mortise and Tenon, breakfast would be devoured before the truck reached the end of the street. "We both have work in the morning."

"We'll be back in time." He put the truck in gear and turned out of her driveway. "Why? You tired?"

"No. I really thought I would be. I can't remember the last time I stayed up all night. I'm always in bed by eleven, up by five, off to work by six. It's almost like…doing this is wrong, you know?" She traced the outline of the house on the corner in the light coating of steam on the window. "I never, ever ditch my responsibilities to go to the beach, just because."

Instead of taking a right, Harlan turned to Sophie, leaning across the truck's interior until he was inches away from her. He tipped her chin, bringing her lips just below his. Sophie's heart hammered in her chest and her pulse began to race. He was going to kiss her again, and the anticipation nearly drove her mad.

"I think you should do more things just because," Harlan said, his voice low and gruff.

"Things—" she let out a breath "—like what?"

"Like this," he said, and lowered his mouth to hers. This kiss was more like a slow waltz, with his lips drifting over hers, his fingers dancing along her jaw. She leaned into him, inhaling the clean, strong scent of him until all she knew, all she cared about was Harlan.

He drew back, but didn't release her. "Now *that* I think you should do all the time." He grinned. "Just because."

She could hardly breathe, hardly think, and yet every ounce of her wanted him to do that again. And again. "That could be dangerous."

His gaze met hers, and even in the dark, she could feel it penetrating beneath the layers of her soul. "Anything between you and I could be dangerous."

They took the Tampa Bay Bridge across the bay, driving all the way over to the Gulf side of Florida. By the time they reached the public beach in Indian Rocks, the sun was just coming up. There was only a handful of cars in the parking lot, and a couple of die-hard beach walkers striding along the sand.

Harlan got out of the truck, grabbing the blanket and cooler as he did. He came around to Sophie's side, and opened her door. All night long, he'd been doing things like that—holding the door for her, pulling out her chair, waiting for her to order first. Grandma Watson would be thrilled. She'd always said the only man worth a woman's time is a gentleman, and tonight, that defined Harlan Jones. Once again, she wondered about the many dimensions to Harlan. As she did, she felt her heart begin to open to him. Dangerous, was the word they'd used before, and that was the only word that came to mind now.

They kicked off their shoes, then walked barefoot on the cool sand, pausing a few feet from shore. A little further down the long expanse of pale, soft sand, a half dozen fishermen stood knee-deep in the water, casting their lines for sharks, flounder and mackerel. Herons and seagulls paced the beach behind them, hoping for cast-offs.

The surf curled in and out with a gentle whoosh. The sun climbed higher in the sky, kissing the water. The tips of the waves glistened in response. Harlan spread out the blanket, settled the picnic basket on one corner, then waited for Sophie to take a seat before he dropped down beside her. Mortise and Tenon bounded off toward the shore, barking and chasing seagulls, and running in and out of the surf.

"This reminds me of mornings in Texas," Harlan said as he leaned back on his elbows. "I've always been an early riser. I like the way the world gets all quiet and…" His voice trailed off as he searched for the right word.

"Hopeful," Sophie said.

"Hopeful," Harlan repeated. "Exactly."

Sophie drew her knees to her chest and wrapped her arms around her legs. "I do too. Most mornings, I walk to work, just to watch the world come awake."

"And help it do that with a whole lotta coffee."

She laughed. "That, too."

They sat there for a while, in a comfortable, pleasant silence, broken only by the occasional cry of a seagull and the soft song of the ocean. The dogs tired of chasing the birds and bounded over to them, sending a spray of water over Sophie. Then they pranced around the blanket, nearly knocking her over in their quest to get closer to the humans.

Harlan laughed. "They like you."

She pushed Mortise back, just before he plopped his big golden tush in her lap. "Too much."

He grinned. "Just give them a chance." He reached into the back pocket of his jeans and pulled out a small bag of dog treats. "Here. Make friends."

"Oh, I don't know if—"

"They don't bite, I swear." He pressed the bag into her hands. "And maybe they'll behave better if they think you're a friend."

Sophie hesitated, then finally relented and took the bag of dog treats. As soon as she opened the top, the dogs caught the scent of the beef-flavored goodies and started dancing all around her, their big bodies practically on top of hers. Being at their level was overwhelming, because it made the dogs seem as big as her. "Whoa, whoa."

Harlan leaned in to her. "Tell them to sit."

"They're not going to listen to me. They never do."

"You have food in your hands. That's a mighty big motivator for a dog. They'll listen."

She cast Harlan a doubtful look, then turned back to the canine terrors. "Uh…sit."

"Say it with authority," he whispered in her ear. "Like you're ordering me around."

She laughed. "You never do what I tell you to either."

"Maybe I haven't been properly motivated." His breath was a warm caress against her neck. Her skin prickled beneath the heat. Damn, that man was sexy.

The dogs barked, jarring Sophie's attention away from Harlan. She fished in the bag for a treat, then looked at Mortise. He seemed to tower over her, and she was sure he weighed at least eighty-five pounds, maybe more. Sophie swallowed hard, then eyed the big dog. "Sit!"

And just like that, Mortise dropped to his haunches. Tenon, seeing there was a reward about to come for her companion, did the same. The two dogs looked at her, panting happily.

Sophie turned to Harlan. "They listened to me!"

"I hate to say it, darlin', but I told you so." He nudged

her elbow. "Now reward them, and they'll be your friends for life."

She flattened her palm and held the treat toward Mortise. He slobbered it right off her hand, then wagged his tail. She did the same for Tenon, who promptly dropped to her paws beside Sophie and put her big golden head on Sophie's knee. "Did you see that?"

"I did indeed." He moved until his chest was against her back, then reached past her to give Tenon an approving pat. "Rub her ears. She likes that."

Sophie reached out a tentative hand, then caressed Tenon's right ear. The dog let out a soft groan and turned her body into the touch. Mortise, jealous of the attention, shoved his snout under Sophie's arm. She laughed and gave him a head rub.

The dogs stayed there for a good ten minutes, lapping up the attention and the occasional treat, until the bag of goodies was gone. Then they scrambled to their feet and went running off in search of more seagulls.

"I had no idea those dogs were so sweet," she said, leaning into Harlan's embrace. "I think I kinda like them."

"As much as you like their owner?" Harlan asked.

She could tell him the truth. That she'd begun to like him more and more over the last few days, that when they finally did have to say goodbye and head off to work, she'd miss him. But she didn't trust these feelings yet.

After all, the Harlan Jones she had spent the night with was the same Harlan Jones who made a living off of embarrassin' moments, as he called them. She tried to keep that front and center in her mind, but every time he touched her, or said her name, or looked at her with those ocean-blue eyes—

She forgot.

"Maybe I should carry biscotti in my pocket," Sophie said. "Then I might get better results with the owner."

"If you did that, darlin', I'd be so obedient and loyal, you'd start calling me Rover."

She laughed. "I'll keep that in mind…Rover."

They sat there for a while, silently watching the surf, looking for the telltale dark hump of a dolphin. So far, the ocean was quiet. Down the beach, one of the fishermen reeled in a foot-long silver fish. A pair of walkers passing by cheered his catch.

"Tell me something," Sophie said.

Harlan reached into the cooler, removed two paper cups, then unscrewed the top of the thermos Sophie had packed and poured them each a cup of coffee. "What?"

"Why are you so dead set against selling that furniture you make?" She thanked him for the coffee, took a sip, then shifted on the blanket until she was facing him. "You're really good, you know."

He'd told Sophie Watson a lot of things tonight, but not the truth about his childhood. Harlan sipped at his coffee, watching the surf, wishing a dolphin would come along and save him from answering.

None did.

"I just don't think it's smart to build a career out of a hobby," he said.

"Why not? I did. I love to entertain and I love to cook. And, breakfast is my favorite meal of the day. Voilà. Coffee shop."

"That's a viable business. Making furniture is too… iffy."

"Plenty of people do it."

"Yeah, well, not me." He sipped at the coffee and watched the surf. And hoped she'd drop the subject.

She didn't. "Not everyone is as talented as you are. I

mean, that furniture you've built is just incredible. And unique. In fact, I was talking to Tobias the other day—"

Any basking in her compliments drew up short when he heard Tobias's name. "You saw my brother?"

She laughed. "Harlan, this is a small town. I see him all the time. He likes coffee and breakfast, too, you know. Specifically mocha lattes and cranberry-orange muffins."

"I didn't know that."

"That's because you only think about work, cowboy. Not breakfast. Me, I think about breakfast almost all day." She pushed her sweatshirt hood back off her face, exposing the golden curls of her hair to the warming sun. Far down the beach, the dogs danced in and out of the water, nipping at the spray bursting off the waves. "Anyway, I never knew he was your brother, not until the other day when he mentioned that his brother was hosting a show on WFFM. We got to talking—"

"About me."

A pink flush filled her cheeks. "About you. And, well, other things."

The flush made him happy in a way he couldn't remember being for a long time. Damn, this woman was starting to grow on him. He knew it was a crazy idea to stay up all night just to see the dolphins swimming by, but every time he'd thought about going home, he found another reason to stay with Sophie.

"Other things?" he teased.

"Other things that are none of your business," she said, a smile curving wide across her face. "Tobias said nobody can make furniture like you can. That the dining-room table you made him gets compliments all the time and deserves to be in a museum."

Harlan shook his head. Tobias had always loved Harlan's

work. He was the only one Harlan ever shared it with, the only one he'd made something for on demand before Sophie Watson came marching into his life, taking his chairs and putting his hobby on display.

That damned dining room table. He'd told Tobias not to say who'd made it, but his little brother, clearly proud, had gone and told Sophie. "My brother is biased."

"I've seen what you've created in that woodshop of yours, and I've been pretty impressed."

He refused to let the praise stick. He had to be smart about his future, and smart didn't involve taking a risk like that. "Thanks, but I think I should stick to my day job."

Her green eyes locked on his. "You're scared."

His gaze went to the surf. Where the hell were those dolphins? "I'm just practical."

"I thought cowboys weren't scared of anything."

"We're scared of plenty. But mostly of mad bulls and demanding women."

She laughed. "Good thing there's none of those here right now."

He arched a brow. "I'd have to disagree. You're about the most demanding woman I know."

"Oh, yeah?" A tease lit her eyes again. For the last few hours, she'd been the Sophie he'd glimpsed throughout the week. And he liked that. Very much. "How about if I demand you kiss me again right now?"

Desire roared through his veins, thundered in his head. He wanted her—wanted her more than he could ever remember wanting anyone before—and he wanted to do a hell of a lot more than kiss her. But they were on a public beach, and he was, at his core, a gentleman. So he leaned over, and gave her a fast, hard kiss.

"That's it?"

"Patience, pardner." He trailed a finger along her lips,

and curbed the urge to press her onto the blanket and taste a lot more than her mouth. "Later, we'll finish what we started."

"Is that a promise?"

He grinned. "That's a date."

Sophie laughed, and curved into his arms. They faced the sea, and a second later, they were rewarded with a trio of dark gray fins, followed by curved, sleek bodies. "The dolphins," Sophie whispered, as if the animals could hear. "They're so beautiful."

"They are," Harlan said, and the two of them leaned forward, watching the graceful animals slice through the water, their backs curving in rhythm, as if they, too, were waves. In seconds, they were gone, disappearing into the deep blue of the ocean.

"We should go," Sophie said. "We have to get back to the real world."

For a while, Harlan had forgotten about his responsibilities. Forgotten about his job. Forgotten about his family. He'd just enjoyed the time with Sophie. "I reckon you're right," he said. But as they packed the picnic away and folded the blanket, he wished she wasn't.

CHAPTER TEN

THE microphone sat in front of Harlan, small, dark and accusatory. He had thirty seconds until he was on the air, and he knew his listeners were going to want a full recap of the Love Lottery day at the carnival.

The trouble was, he couldn't think of a single funny line. Or a way to twist that moment on the Tilt-A-Whirl, or any of the other incredible ones that had followed that night and the next morning on the beach, into a joke.

More than that, he didn't want to. He wanted to hold those moments, preserve them in his memory, take them out from time to time. Hell, right now, he wanted to do it all again. Have Sophie crushed to his chest, then hold her in the dark and kiss her until they both had to come up for air.

He'd spent the entire night and part of the morning with Sophie, and all he wanted right now was more time. For the first time in his life, he wanted to call in sick, ditch the show, the job, the lists, and head down to Cuppa Java Café—just to see her smile at him. He wanted to haul her out to those chairs, and spend the day right beside her, listening to her talk and seeing the world of Edgerton Shores through her eyes. And he didn't want to share a word of it with his listeners.

Damn, that woman sure had gotten under his skin. And he wasn't so sure he wanted that to change.

He sighed. Did he have a choice, really? Tobias was counting on him to bring WFFM back from the dead. Harlan couldn't let his brother down.

On the other side of the glass separating him and his producer, Carl gave Harlan the countdown to start. The opening music played in Harlan's headphones, and he scooted his chair closer to the mike. "Welcome to *Horsin' Around with Harlan!* Got quite the show for ya'll today. The Love Doctor will be in after the eight o'clock news report, to answer all your questions about that pesky emotion called love. Until then, I want to hear about your favorite getaway spots in the Tampa Bay area. No Love Lottery talk today. I'm sure you're all plumb tired of my dating jokes anyway. So call me with your getaway ideas. I'll be right back after this word from our sponsor."

From inside the production booth, Carl gave Harlan a confused look. "What the hell are you doing?" Carl said into Harlan's earpiece.

"Shaking things up."

Carl shrugged, then signaled that there was a caller on the line. The commercial ended, and Harlan did his intro, then pressed the button to answer the call.

"Welcome to the show," Harlan looked down at the computer, "Joe."

"Hi, Harlan. I'm Joe Johnson, with the *Tampa Bay News.* I had a few questions for you."

Harlan chuckled. "Well, this ain't an interview show." He reached for the disconnect button.

"I just wanted to get a quote or two on how your dates have been going."

That, Harlan figured, he could do. Maybe drum up

a little publicity for the cause the Love Lottery was supporting at the same time. Sophie would like that.

"We had a nice time." It had been more than nice. Sexy, fun, and memorable. But he stuck to the neutrality of nice. Still keeping the memories and the highlights close to his chest.

Joe laughed. "Nice? My readers want some details. Come on, Harlan, share a little."

"Sorry. I don't have a whole lotta time to share the details anyway. We've got other ground to cover on the show today." Which was a lie, because he had four hours of airtime to fill and only he chose how to fill it. Harlan had been on the air for nearly ten years now, and he had never outright lied to his audience. He might have exaggerated a detail or two, beefed up a story to make it funnier, but he'd never held back details like this. Was he getting soft? Or was he...

Falling for her?

Not a decision he could make right now. "We had a busy night at the carnival. Both of us working and all," Harlan went on. "Sophie had to run the ticket booth and I had to pop in and update my listeners from time to time. That's one of the hazards of two headstrong stallions trying to find time in the same corral."

"Is that what you're thinking of doing with Sophie? Spending time in the same corral?"

"We're just dating for the week." He didn't need to give this guy anything more than that.

"And after the week is over?"

"I'm just taking it one day at a time," he said, which was the truth. They'd had a great night together, one he wasn't going to forget anytime soon, but when it came to forever...well, that was a whole other rodeo. "Now, if you have any other questions about the community wellness center or—"

"So do you like her?"

He bit back a curse. Somehow, the tables had gotten turned on him, and he'd become the interviewee on his own show. He glanced at the clock. Ernie wasn't due in for another thirty minutes. Seven minutes remained in the segment, and Carl was grinning like a fool, because Harlan Jones had just sidestepped into his own hot seat.

What was he supposed to say? The truth? Hell, yes, he liked her. But he also knew Sophie was a woman who deserved, and wanted, more than a cowboy who spun in and out of her life like a tornado. She was the kind of woman a man settled down with. Harlan looked around the studio, thinking of all the work still to be done at WFFM to get it back into the black, and knew he couldn't promise to be that man. Not right now.

"Sophie Watson is a wonderful woman," he said. "I'm sure some lucky man is going to scoop her up and make her his wife."

Saying the words hurt. For a minute there last night, he'd imagined he could be the man who did that. Pictured himself sitting on blankets with her for the rest of their lives, watching dolphins in the morning and sunsets at night. But as soon as he'd walked into WFFM, he'd remembered his responsibilities, and every time the thought of Sophie in his arms arose in his mind, he reminded himself of where his duty lay.

Take care of your brother, his mother had said, the last words she'd ever said, and he'd promised her he always would. Just like he had when they were little.

If there was ever a time when his brother needed him to be a caretaker, it was now. And that meant a personal life had to go on hold.

"Some guy almost did make Sophie his wife," Joe said. "A local politician, in fact."

"Really?" This was a new fact, something he hadn't known before. Not that he should be surprised. A beautiful woman like Sophie had undoubtedly captured more than a few hearts over the years. Nevertheless, a surge of jealousy rose in his chest.

"I'm betting, since you're new in town, that you don't know the story."

Harlan glanced at Carl, hoping there'd be another caller waiting, which would give him an excuse to get this guy off the line. But there were no other people waiting, and six minutes of airtime to fill before the commercial break. "I'm sure you've got some tall tale to share, pardner, but—"

"She ran out on her own wedding. Hurried out of the church so fast, you would have thought her dress was on fire. I know. I saw the whole thing. The media started calling her Cold Feet Coffeegirl after that." Joe chuckled. "She got more press than a presidential election."

Sophie had run out of her own wedding? She'd never mentioned that to him. Cold feet? Or wrong groom?

Surely she'd had a good reason. The entertainer in him wanted to know why. The man who'd made a promise outside the Tilt-A-Whirl held back from asking. He stared at the silver head of the microphone, and decided no amount of ratings was worth splashing Sophie's private life across the airwaves. "I'm sure that's ancient history. Folks, we're still looking for your favorite Tampa getaway, so give me a call if—"

"A year isn't ancient history," Joe interrupted with a chuckle. "Seems Miss Sophie gets cold feet, so I hope you aren't planning a wedding."

The man's derogatory tone sent a flash of anger through

Harlan. He tamped it down. Exploding on air wasn't the smartest career move he could make. "What I do with my private life, and for that matter, what Sophie does with hers, isn't up for discussion. Thank you for calling."

"Hypocrite."

Harlan's finger hovered over the disconnect button. Why didn't he just hang up on the guy?

"You talk about how open you are with your audience, how you want them to know all about Harlan Jones, but when someone calls and asks you some hard questions, you clam right up."

"Parts of my life aren't open to the public. Plain and simple." Harlan signaled Carl to cue up a commercial. He didn't care which one, as long as it got this guy off the air. "Well, Mr. Johnson, I hate to interrupt you, but I need to cut to commercial."

"You don't want to hear more about Sophie Watson's engagement?"

Harlan hit the disconnect button on the call. That man had said damned near enough. "This is Harlan Jones, and you're listening to *Horsin' Around with Harlan.* We'll be back in a few, so stay tuned."

And when we come back, we sure as hell ain't talking about Sophie. Or me.

That was a conversation he was going to have with Sophie herself. Damned soon.

CHAPTER ELEVEN

SOPHIE gave her grandmother a kiss on the cheek, catching a whiff of the light floral scent of Grandma Watson's perfume. Sophie hated to leave, but she had to get to work. Mornings were the busiest time at Cuppa Java Café, and poor Lulu was managing the shop alone right now. "You sure you're going to be okay?"

Grandma patted her hand. "You worry too much. I'll be fine. Now go to work."

Sophie cast a doubtful eye over her grandmother's thin, wiry frame. To Sophie, she seemed as delicate as a sapling, as fragile as a crystal vase. Grandma had called early this morning, not long after Sophie said goodbye to Harlan, to ask where Sophie had put her broom because she'd dropped a glass on the hard tile floor of the kitchen. Sophie had told her not to move, that she'd be over right away to clean up the mess. She'd run all the way to Grandma's house, so sure her stubborn grandmother would try to clean the mess up herself, and end up slipping and falling. Just as Sophie feared, she'd found Grandma in the kitchen, wielding the broom.

A half hour and a long lecture about being safe later, Sophie had cleaned up the mess. She'd made Grandma breakfast, and stirred together some tuna salad for

Grandma's lunch later. "Promise to call me if you need anything."

"I will," Grandma said. "Now go. You have a long day ahead of you, dear."

Sophie gave her grandmother another kiss, then headed for the front door. Worry still nagged at her, but she couldn't stay here all day. She did have a long day, as Grandma had said. One that would culminate with the town dance, the finale for the Love Lottery and the Spring Fling.

And the same place where she'd see Harlan again. Her heart nearly sang at the prospect. The smile brimming inside her curved across her face. She thought of being with him last night, of him kissing her, of his arms around her on the beach this morning. Of the magical moment when they'd seen the dolphins. Over the last week, she'd seen a new side of Harlan Jones. One she liked. Very much.

It took ten minutes to walk to the shop from her grand-mother's house, and Sophie used the time to enjoy the Florida sunshine.

A few days ago, Harlan Jones had accused her of not taking time to enjoy her slice of paradise down here on the Gulf coast. And even though she hated to admit it, he was right, and she was darn glad he'd talked her into going to the beach early this morning. After last night, and the crazy, spontaneous time they'd had, she'd realized she *had* been working a ridiculous number of hours—and spending what free time she had taking care of her grandmother. No spontaneous shopping trips, no vacations, no dating. It was little wonder someone had to force her into going out on a date. She would have to remember to thank Mildred.

She neared the shop, and her gaze settled on the two chairs Harlan had made. Beneath them sat two footstools, made out of the same wood nailed in slats that curved over an arched base. She smiled.

He must have left them here this morning, after he'd brought her home and before he went to work. He'd never said a word that he'd been working on them or that they were done. Instead, he'd put them out as a surprise. The footstools were as beautiful as the chairs, and she wondered again why he didn't just try to make a living at something he so clearly excelled at.

Harlan Jones excelled at a lot of things, Sophie thought. Her fingers went to her lips. A lot of things.

That man was starting to grow on her. Well, honestly, he was doing much more than that. In the last few days, he'd pretty much been her only thought in between steaming milk and mixing dough. Him, his sexy drawl and his electric kisses. Tonight, she'd see Harlan again. A week ago, she would have dreaded the encounter but today—

Well, today had her wondering what she should wear. If she should leave her hair down or put it up. Whether he would smile when he saw her, whisper something sweet in her ear. How long it would be before he asked her to dance. What it would be like to take a twirl around the dance floor wrapped in his arms. And most of all, whether he would kiss her again. Or maybe do more.

Still dreaming of the night ahead, she headed inside Cuppa Java Café. Tonight she'd wear a sexy little dress, put her hair up and pull those high heels out of her closet. She could hardly wait to see his reaction.

"Well, Mr. Johnson, I hate to interrupt you, but I need to cut to commercial." Harlan's voice greeted her as soon as she walked in the door.

"You don't want to hear more about Sophie Watson's engagement?" said his caller. Sophie froze.

"This is Harlan Jones, and you're listening to *Horsin'*

Around with Harlan. We'll be back in a few, so stay tuned."

The words took a second to register in Sophie's brain. Harlan's voice. Coming from the shop's loudspeakers. A dozen people hanging on every word, several of them laughing softly.

Lulu came out from the back of the shop, two gallons of milk in her hands. "Hey, Sophie."

"Don't hey me. Why is that station on inside here?"

Confusion filled Lulu's features. "I thought we were pro-Harlan now. And I thought it'd be nice for you to hear his voice when you came in to—"

"I don't want to hear that man's voice ever again." Sophie switched the station, settling on an upbeat country music tune. It could have been opera for all she cared— anything other than the man who had just betrayed her.

Harlan had promised. He'd looked her right in the eyes and swore he wouldn't plaster her private life all over the radio. Then he'd gone and made her fall for him, with all those kisses and his kindness to her grandmother, and that dolphin idea, and those hours of talking. She'd thought he cared. Thought maybe they were building something real.

When all Harlan had been building was his plan to increase ratings.

Sophie's heart ached, the pain deeper than any she had ever known before. He had betrayed her, and she had been foolish enough to fall for him. Once again, she'd been too starry-eyed to see the truth, and ended up a media punch line. Harlan Jones was no better than a snake in the grass.

"You okay, hun?" Lulu asked, resting a hand on Sophie's shoulder.

"Fine." Sophie figured she could lie as well as Harlan.

Then she headed into the back of the shop before the tears that had begun to brim in her eyes cascaded down her face.

Harlan was sweating by the time he left the station's booth later that morning. Every damned caller he'd had wanted to talk about the local scandal with Sophie Watson. He'd done his best to switch the subject, but these people were like ticks on a hound dog—relentless. He wondered if she'd heard the show, then remembered she didn't listen to WFFM. Hopefully he could get over to the coffee shop today and tell her what had happened before she heard it from someone else.

He turned down Ernie's offer for an early lunch, headed into his brother's office and shut the door. The work still sat in a pile on the desk—invoices to go over, bills to pay, guests to book.

He came around the desk, sat down and started tackling the pile. The sooner he was done, the sooner he could go to Sophie's shop and get the rest of the story from her. If that reporter was right, and Sophie's broken engagement had been big news, that surely explained her reluctance to get out in the public eye.

He was knee-deep in work when he heard a knock on his door. He looked up to see Tobias standing in the doorway. "Hey, little brother." Harlan took in the sweat beading on Tobias's brow—probably from using the crutches to get all the way from the parking lot to the office at the end of the hall—and the slight flush in his cheeks. "Shouldn't you be at home resting?"

Tobias waved off the question and entered the room. His crutches made soft plopping sounds against the carpet, but it seemed to Harlan that he was leaning on them a bit less than before. Tobias settled into one of the visitors' chairs, propped the crutches against the side, then leaned forward. "How long are you going to keep doing this?"

"Doing what?"

"Everything. I am cleared to come back to work, part-time. That means I should be sitting behind that desk, instead of you, but every time I try to put in a few hours, you send me home like I'm two years old."

Harlan put down his pen and let out a sigh. "I just don't want you to end up in the hospital again. You could get another infection, or get hurt walking around with those crutches or—"

"Will you quit worrying about me? I'm old enough to do it for myself." Tobias put up a hand to stop Harlan's protests. "I appreciate you coming out here to help me get the station back on track and also taking care of everything while I was in the hospital. I truly do. But you don't have to mother hen me for the rest of my life."

"I'm not. I'm just—"

"You are. When you were in Texas, you did it from afar. Called me all the time, sent me money whenever I got behind, even cosigned for my loan to buy this place."

Harlan scowled. "I should have done more than that."

"What more? You did plenty."

"You asked me, back when you started, to come out here and help you get the place off the ground. I was too damned wrapped up in my own show to say yes. I should have. If I had then maybe—" Harlan's gaze went to the crutches again.

"Maybe, what? You'd save me from my own irresponsibility?"

"This place would have been running smoothly if I came out here when you first asked. And maybe you wouldn't have been so worried about it you wouldn't have gotten distracted on that boat—"

Tobias let out a sharp laugh. "Harlan, I got distracted because I had a few too many beers. Not because of work. You know me. I'm more play than work."

"I could have taken some of this off your shoulders," Harlan said. His gaze went back to Tobias's cast and guilt rocked him. "You're hurting financially. If I had been here, maybe that wouldn't have happened."

Tobias sighed. "There's a fine line between helping and hurting. You mean well, Harlan, I know you do, but you gotta let me succeed and fail on my own." He shook his head. "I know, half of this is my fault. I keep on asking for help, instead of taking my own chances. Ditched responsibilities because I knew you would take up the slack and send me a few bucks to cover me. I guess I just got used to you looking out for me."

"You're my little brother. I'm supposed to look out for you."

"And you're supposed to let me grow up, too. The best thing you ever did was tell me no years before. And the best thing you can do now is quit helping me."

"I…" Harlan let out a breath. He thought of all the years he had bailed Tobias out—whether it was with money or with advice—always, always looking out for his little brother. Even now, with Tobias nearing thirty, Harlan looked at him and saw the kid he used to be, not the man he'd become. "I've always meant well."

"I know you did. And I think it just got to be a…habit. You took care of all of us, all our lives, Harlan. Hell, you worked so many hours it was a wonder you had time to go to school. And you're still doing it."

"Dad needs financial support. He doesn't have beans for retirement."

"Even Dad can take care of himself. I think you'll find that if you let go of the reins, the horse will naturally find its way home. It might get lost a couple times, but it'll eventually get there." Tobias got to his feet, came around the desk and tugged Harlan's chair away from the desk. His blue eyes, so like Harlan's, showed a strength and determination Harlan had never noticed before. "This time, I'm taking the reins from you. Now, let me sit at my desk and get some work done."

"But—"

"But nothing. I have screwed up a lot over the last few years, and I know it. Spending a lot of time in a hospital room gives you plenty of time to think. And realize a few truths about yourself. I've been relying on you too damned long. It's time I got serious and took care of myself."

Harlan stared at his brother. He wasn't sure what to say. For as long as he could remember, he'd been the worrier. The caretaker. He'd put food on his family's table and made sure their bills were covered. Now Tobias was telling him to stop?

"I know what you love to do, but you're too damned stubborn to do it," Tobias said. "If I let you, you'd keep on doing all those other things instead of going home to that woodshop and being…happy."

"I'm happy."

"You're *existing,* Harlan. There's a difference. You can't tell me you love working in radio."

"It's my job, Tobias."

"That doesn't answer the question."

Harlan sighed. "Okay, yeah, I'll admit it. Lately, I haven't been as…invested in my show as I should be. I guess it's gotten old."

"Or maybe you're finally starting to realize that all the work in the world doesn't make up for the fact that you're not doing what you love."

Harlan glanced at the poster on the wall, an eighteenby-thirty-inch advertisement the station had designed to promote Harlan's show. His own face smiled back at him from the corner, but for some reason, the image didn't look like himself. It looked…fake.

Was Tobias right? Was Harlan pouring himself into his job to avoid doing the one thing he really loved to do?

"Making a living off a hobby is foolish," Harlan said. "Look at Dad."

"Dad wasn't smart enough to get a regular job until he made his hobby work. He didn't have health insurance and a 401k and a long-range plan, like you do. You're smart, Harlan. And responsible as hell. If for some reason the furniture business didn't work out, you'd do what it took to keep the income coming in."

"Yeah, but—"

"Don't but me. And don't let the mistakes of our father keep you from living the life you were meant to live. It's time you took care of *you,* big brother." Tobias leaned on the back of Harlan's chair. "So I'm kicking you out of here, and in the process, forcing you to have free time. What you do with it is up to you."

Harlan looked up at his younger brother and saw him with new eyes. He was a man now, one who was taking charge, hell, even telling Harlan what to do. It was time to stop seeing Tobias as anything other than the scared, hungry little boy who had relied on his big brother to take care of him. "You're as crazy as a flying pig. I'm not going into the furniture business."

"You are and you should." Tobias pulled the chair out further, nearly tipping Harlan out of it. He gave his older brother a wide, but firm grin. "Now get the hell out of my office before I have to get the cattle prod."

"I'm not going."

Mildred turned to Grandma Watson. Both women were

already dressed for the evening, in beaded dresses and low-heeled shoes. Mildred, in typical Mildred fashion, wore bright pink, complete with a pink-and-white wrist corsage—a gift from Art Conway. "Maybe if I hit her with pepper spray, she'll be more cooperative."

"You are not pepper spraying my only granddaughter, Mildred Meyers." Grandma put a fist on her hip. "Sophie's upset. She just needs a moment."

"I don't need a moment. I'm not going to the dance."

Mildred raised a brow, as if to say, *see? I told you so.*

Grandma sighed, grabbed another cookie from the plate, then ate two bites before she spoke again. "I understand that man did something that you think is unforgivable."

"*Think?* It is. He promised me he wouldn't say one more word about my private life on the air. Then I hear him telling the whole world about how I ran out on my own wedding—"

"Sophie, I hardly think WFFM reaches the whole world," Mildred cut in.

"A big enough portion of it." Sophie turned to the breadbox, pulled out a box of biscotti, and took one of the cookies. Just before she took a bite, she remembered they were Harlan's favorite treat, and she put it back inside the container.

"You're holding out on us." Grandma pouted. "You had biscotti all this time, and didn't share it with us?"

Sophie put the box on the table. "Here you are. Eat them all. Please." Then maybe she wouldn't be reminded of Harlan and the appealing way he said *bis-yummy.*

"We can't eat biscotti without coffee," Grandma said, then gave her granddaughter a sweet smile. "Especially that amazing coffee you make."

"I still can't believe my matchmaking instincts were so off," Mildred said while Sophie began grinding beans and setting up the coffeepot. "I really saw Harlan as the perfect match for Sophie."

Grandma patted Mildred's hand. "It could still work out."

Sophie didn't tell the women the chances of that were zero. She'd nearly married a man she didn't love because she'd fooled herself into thinking he was the one, that he actually cared and supported what was important to her. She wasn't going to be a fool a second time, not with her heart. Not again.

A few minutes later, Sophie had freshly brewed Guatemalan Roast poured into three mugs. With biscotti in her hand and coffee in her mug, Mildred stopped talking about using her pepper spray, thank goodness. Maybe they'd both forgotten the crazy idea of convincing Sophie that going to the dance was a good idea.

"You better hurry," Grandma said, after her third biscotti and second cup of coffee. "Or you won't be ready in time."

Apparently they hadn't forgotten. Sophie sighed.

"Your grandmother's right," Mildred said. "Besides, you, of all people, can't be late." The older lady smiled, and in that moment, Sophie saw that she had been holding back a trump card all this time. "You're the one making the speech, thanking the volunteers and announcing how much money we raised for the community wellness center."

Another speech. Sophie groaned. "Mildred, really, anyone can do that."

"No, not just anyone can. You're passionate about this, Sophie." Beside Mildred, Grandma Watson nodded her agreement. "No one can make the case for this center like you can."

"Miss Meyers…" Sophie's voice trailed off. The two women had a point. They sat at Sophie's kitchen table, watching her expectantly and waiting for her to see it. Sophie sighed. When it came right down to it, the need for a town community wellness center trumped everything else, even her dread of giving speeches and her worry that every newspaper in a tri-state area would be there to dredge up the past. "You're right."

"Of course we are." Mildred cheered. "Now go get your party dress on."

Grandma nodded. "Show that Harlan Jones what he's missing out on."

"And if he tries to hurt our Sophie again," Mildred said, digging in her purse for the ubiquitous spray can that went everywhere with her, "I'll take him out."

Harlan spent the afternoon at the park with the dogs. When the volunteer crews came in to set up the temporary stage for the band and string twinkle lights in the trees, he took Mortise and Tenon home. Instead of bounding up to the house, though, the dogs headed for the woodshop.

He chuckled. The goldens knew him too well. They had undoubtedly read the stress in his shoulders and guessed he'd be working it off with some wood and a hammer. Either that or Tobias had been talking to them.

Mortise and Tenon bounced on their paws and barked in tandem, waiting until he lifted the garage door and the three of them could go inside. As soon as the door cleared the ground, the dogs squeezed underneath and bounded off to their favorite spots—Mortise by the tool bench, Tenon in the corner. Harlan flicked the light switch, and started to walk toward the table saw.

He stopped. Took in the pieces that sat in various stages of completion. Another pair of chairs like the ones at Sophie's shop. A coffee table made of a rich mahogany, its squat legs carved in an Old World pattern that matched the elaborate drawers and thick weight of the long rectangular piece. A bookshelf that was to go in Tobias's den, and would match the other minimalist Shaker style pieces he'd already constructed for his brother.

All these years, he'd never seen the pieces he created en masse, never seen them as a...future. He finally let the words he'd been hearing for years sink in, and take root. *Incredible work. Unique designs. True talent.*

Then Sophie's words on the beach came back to him. *I thought cowboys weren't scared of anything.*

He ran a hand over the top of the bookshelf. His palm slipped along the sleek wood, sanded as smooth as glass. The piece seemed to whisper to him. *Take a chance. Risk it all. You can do it.*

Then his mind filled with the images of his childhood—the empty bank account, the lean meals, the threadbare clothes. The hours Harlan had worked, the pitifully small checks he'd handed over to his mother, trying to do what he could to alleviate the stress in her features, the heavy burden on her shoulders. Harlan had worried—worried enough for all of them.

And in the background, the father who tried and failed, tried and failed, all at the expense of his own family. That was where dreams got people.

Harlan took his hand off the bookshelf. He called the dogs to him, shut up the woodshop for tonight, and headed into the house.

Sophie's doorbell rang. Twice, in short succession. Goodness, Grandma and Mildred were persistent. They'd only left ten minutes ago, and already they were back? She hadn't even had time to get dressed yet.

Sophie drew on a robe, knotted the belt, then crossed to

her front door and opened it. "Harlan. What are you doing here?"

Harlan shifted from foot to foot, then removed his hat and held it to his chest. If he was going to the town dance, it didn't show in his attire—he was wearing jeans and a T-shirt advertising the radio station. She was tempted to shut the door in his face—after all that had happened he dared to come by her house?—but she waited. For what, she wasn't sure.

"I came by to apologize," he said.

The anger that had bloomed in her chest when she saw him on her porch began to dissipate. A little. "For what?"

"I stopped by the coffee shop a little while ago. Talked to Lulu. Got the whole scoop on your wedding, or, non-wedding, I guess."

Now the anger flared again, a hot flame racing through her. "Great. Now you can share all the gory details with your listeners." She went to shut the door, but Harlan grabbed it and stopped her.

"Let me say my piece, Sophie."

"Don't you think you've said enough? Told enough of my life to all your loyal fans? And given the reporters something to write about?"

"That was never my intention. That reporter brought it up, and I swear—"

She put up a hand, cutting him off. "I don't want to hear the excuses, Harlan. You don't have any idea the kind of damage you leave in your wake."

He took a step closer to her, making her acutely aware she was only wearing a robe. Damn the man for still being able to affect her. "I admit, in the beginning, I shouldn't have told those lunatic neighbor stories. I have apologized for that, and stopped telling any tales about you. But the whole thing about your engagement was an accident. I didn't exploit it and I didn't exploit you."

"No, you just turned me into the laughingstock of the town. Again. Do you have any idea what my life was like after I ran out of that church? How the reporter vultures hounded me? How everyone focused on that instead of my coffee shop? People came into the shop and didn't want to order coffee, they wanted to get a scoop. It took months for that to stop. *Months.*"

"I'm sorry. I had no idea." He reached for her, but she leaned away from his touch.

"Leave me alone, Harlan. Just go away."

"Why are you so afraid?"

Her chin jutted up. "I'm not afraid of anything."

"You are, darlin'," he said, that smooth drawl washing over her even as she wished he'd stop talking. "You're afraid of making a public spectacle. You're afraid that people will talk about you and your mistakes from here to Kingdom Come. And you're afraid as hell to fall in love."

"You're wrong." But the lie was getting harder to hold on to. No matter how many times her friends had told her not to let the wedding fiasco bother her, she had. She had let it stop her from being her usual self. From getting out in public and really supporting the community wellness center.

She had been afraid, and what had it cost her?

"When we were on the radio and you kissed me that afternoon, were you afraid?" Harlan asked.

"Well, I hardly had time to think about anything. It just…happened." Because she'd wanted it even more than the crowd had. Because she'd been unable to see or hear anything other than Harlan.

"Exactly. You just did it. You didn't think about the

consequences. If you ask me, and I know you aren't, but I'm telling you what I think anyway, you've gotten yourself all wrapped up in the possibilities, rather than living with the actualities."

"What's that supposed to mean?"

"You keep on worrying about what might happen instead of noticing what did."

Oh, she had noticed all right. She'd gone and fallen for a man who was as wrong for her as a dress on an elephant. "Who are you to talk? You're so afraid to go into business for yourself that you keep working a job that you don't like."

"That's different." He scowled. "I have people depending on me. I can't just up and take a risk like that."

She propped a fist on her hip. "Seems to me you keep on worrying about what might happen instead of concentrating on what did."

He scowled. "Dammit, that's not the same thing."

"Yeah, it is, Harlan. You want me to take risks, to trust you, and you don't even trust yourself." She bit her lip, wishing he would leave. "I *did* take a risk. I trusted you. And look where it got me."

"It got you right here. Doing things that were maybe out of your comfort zone, but they were good for you."

She looked away, cursing the tears that blurred her vision. "You don't know what's good for me. You just do your show and you don't think about the consequences. About the people you hurt with your words."

"I used to be that way," Harlan said. "Then I met you."

Her gaze swiveled back to his. She wanted to believe him—everything within her wanted to do that—but she couldn't. She'd been fooled once before, and come within minutes of walking down the aisle to a man who had fed her lines about how much he loved and supported her, when at heart, he didn't. He'd only thought about his own self, his own career. "I don't believe you. You told me yourself that your job is to entertain listeners and up the ratings. To make money, no matter who gets hurt in the process. When it comes right down to it, which is more important, the bottom line or the people you care about?"

"That's not a fair question, Sophie. I'm supporting—"

"The bottom line." She shook her head. "I knew it. You know what? Don't bother coming to the dance tonight. Just tell everyone the Cold Feet Coffeegirl stood you up. Your listeners should get a real kick out of that one. Goodbye, Harlan."

This time she did shut the door. And he didn't try to stop her.

CHAPTER TWELVE

THE band was playing a medley of pop hits, the music amplified by the wide leaves of the palm trees, sending sounds skipping from one end of the park to the other. People began to trickle into the park, many of them couples Mildred had put together. They were walking hand in hand, or arm in arm. Sophie spied Lulu and Kevin heading for the buffet line and sent them a friendly wave. Lulu was acting like she couldn't care less if Kevin was with her, but every once in a while she snuck a glance over her shoulder to see if he was still following her. When she turned back, her face held a soft, secret smile. Kevin just grinned, more than happy to play along.

Sophie glanced down at the soft jersey black dress and heels she'd chosen for the dance—partly because Mildred and Grandma Watson rejected her first dozen outfits. It was one of those figure-hugging dresses that she had bought on a whim, then left to hang in her closet, waiting for the perfect occasion. Well, really, waiting for an occasion when she felt brave enough to wear it.

The dress was a big step out of Sophie's regular attire. It had a deep plunging V neckline, a narrow waist and a pencil skirt that took some getting used to, particularly when she had to walk in the four-inch heels that Grandma and Mildred had insisted were the only footwear option for such a dress. Thankfully, there were concrete paths winding all around the park, which made walking a lot easier.

Lulu crossed to her and let out a low whistle. "Sister, that is a dress and a half. You look like a supermodel."

Sophie ran a hand down the dress, suddenly feeling uncomfortable and very, very noticeable. So much for her plan to blend into the background. "Thanks. I don't know what I was thinking. It's too much for tonight."

"That dress," Lulu said, pointing a finger at Sophie's attire, "is too much *anytime*. And that's why it's perfect for you."

"For me? Lulu, I'm no sex kitten." She held up one high-heeled foot. "And I never wear shoes like these."

"Well, you should. It looks terrific on you." Lulu crossed her arms over her chest. "So why did you wear it then?"

"It's been sitting in my closet forever and I thought it was time I got my money's worth out of it."

Lulu laughed. "You are such a liar. You wanted to be noticed. Particularly by that cowboy."

Sophie shook her head. "Not by him. That's for sure."

"Well, it's going to get people talking, that's for sure."

Sophie raised her chin. "Let 'em talk." She thought about all the months she had worried about what people were thinking. Worried about how it would impact her business. Worried about…well, about nothing, really. Yeah, it might have been better to do it before she was halfway down the aisle, but truly, her decision not to marry Jim was all hers. Didn't matter what anyone else thought. "I'm done worrying about what people think."

"I'm sure glad to hear that, girlfriend." Then Lulu glanced over and saw Kevin, who sent her a little wave. "Speaking of getting noticed, I need to get back to my honey bunny."

"You and Kevin really seem to have hit it off."

Lulu's smile was wide and full. "That boy put the sprinkles back on my ice cream. But don't tell him I said that."

"Why not?"

"Because keeping him on his toes keeps him busy trying to woo me. And, girl, I deserve to be wooed." Lulu winked, then headed off to Kevin's side. By the time she got there, the wide smile had been curbed, and she was wearing an attitude of I-don't-care, so transparent men on the moon could have seen through it.

Sophie headed toward the podium set up in the gazebo. In a few minutes, she'd make her final speech, and this time, it had to count. Over the course of the week, the committee had raised several thousand dollars through contributions and Spring Fling activity fees. It was enough to get the renovations on the building at least started. With one more big push, maybe there'd be enough to see the project through to completion.

And if there wasn't, well, she'd find another way to spread the word and raise the money. The town needed this, and Sophie was done letting her fears get in the way of her dreams.

She took a deep breath, then crossed to the podium. Earlier, she'd put her speech notes on the stand, and she pulled them in front of her now and reviewed the high points. She noticed a second microphone attached to the podium, this one bearing the bright green and white logo for WFFM.

Tobias crutched his way over to her. The color and excitement in his face told her he was feeling better. "It was Harlan's idea," he said, pointing at the mike. "He called me up a little while ago, told me to get the remote crew down here and do a live broadcast. He thought it would be good to give your cause a little extra exposure."

"He did?"

Tobias leaned on the podium, taking some of the weight off his leg. "I don't know if you caught the whole show today, but he did his damndest to get people to talk about something other than you. It's live radio, you know, so you can't always control what comes out of people's mouths." He tapped the top of the podium. "Anyway, I'll let you get to your speech. I gotta get over to the remote booth and make sure we're all set to stream live."

After Tobias left, Sophie considered what he'd said. Had she jumped to conclusions with Harlan? Assumed the worst about him because it was easier than hearing she was wrong? And less scary than letting him into her heart?

She'd always thought of herself as a risk-taker—she'd gone into business for herself, after all—but maybe she hadn't been taking the most important kinds of risks. The kind where she allowed another person to get close to her.

When it came to Harlan, though, the risk seemed too big. She'd trusted him, and ended up hurt.

Tobias gave her the go-signal. Sophie cleared her throat, then started to speak. "I'd like to welcome everyone to the annual Spring Fling dance. Tonight, we have the added excitement of it being the last official date for our Love Lottery couples. I hope you all had a wonderful and romantic week." A cheer went up among the crowd. "We held the Love Lottery, not just to give happy endings to eligible singles, but to help make another dream come true. This community is important to me, as I'm sure it is to all of you. You all have been there for me, for my business, and for my grandmother, over the last few years, and I wanted to say thank you. If it hadn't been for that support, I don't think I would have been brave enough to take the risks that I have."

As she said the words, she realized they were true. Yes, there were a few mean-spirited people and reporters who had branded her with that nickname after she ran out on her wedding, but by and large it was the people of Edgerton Shores—her friends, her family—who had hugged her and supported her. Who had stopped in at Cuppa Java Café, some every day, to show their support for her business, one cup of coffee at a time.

"I'm asking you now to support each other. This town needs a community wellness center, a place where people young and old can go to take exercise classes, play games, and most of all, build that support network that all of us need. For a long time, having a community wellness center in Edgerton Shores was just a dream, but now, thanks to the community's help, we're that much closer to making it a reality. That's what makes Edgerton Shores a town that people love to call home. A place I love to call home."

The crowd cheered. Sophie's gaze roamed across the familiar faces. Her heart skipped a beat when she saw one she hadn't expected.

Harlan.

He stood at the edge of the crowd, watching her. She couldn't read his expression from this far away, but could feel the intensity of his gaze, all the way to her toes. She had to force herself to look away, to concentrate on her speech. He had come to the dance, but that didn't mean he'd come for her.

"Thank you all," she said, "for supporting the community wellness center, and for being a part of Edgerton Shores' Spring Fling celebration. And for those of you participating in the Love Lottery, I wish you a happy ending."

Then she got off the stage, because her throat had clogged and her eyes had started burning. Happy endings all around...except for Sophie herself.

The band started playing again, this time a slow song, encouraging the couples to come onto the gazebo and take a spin. Volunteers carried the podium away, just as several couples stepped into their partners' arms, under the twinkling lights strung around the circular world of the gazebo.

Sophie headed for the drinks table, and grabbed herself a glass of punch, downing the fruity drink fast. Her nerves hadn't totally disappeared during that speech, but they had abated. From now on, she was determined not to let her nervousness stop her when it came to raising the funds for the center.

Ernie came up to her, wearing a bright red Love Doctor emblazoned suit with a white shirt and white shoes. "Hell of a speech there," he said.

"Thanks."

"In fact, you inspired me. What says love more than supporting a community?" He reached in his breast pocket and with a flourish, pulled out a check.

"Oh, my. Thank you!" Sophie stared at the generous numbers. "This will be a huge help. You have no idea."

He shrugged. "I make enough money telling people how to be happy with each other. It's only right I give some of that back."

"Edgerton Shores truly appreciates your generosity." She reached out and drew Ernie into a quick hug.

He laughed. "Does this mean I'm forgiven for making you kiss Harlan?"

She glanced at the check again, still not believing the numbers before her. "Yes, completely."

"Good. Because I think you and he especially deserve that happy ending you were talking about." Ernie jerked his head to the right. Harlan was striding toward them, a tall drink of whiskey as Lulu called him, in dark jeans, a white button-down shirt and that white cowboy hat. "I guess you don't have to wait too long to hear what kind of ending you're getting."

Damn. Even now, just the sight of Harlan made her melt. She wanted to leave, to avoid what was coming, but decided the new Sophie, the one who didn't care what people said about her, would stand her ground. Ernie said goodbye to her, then walked away.

"You've got a way with words, darlin'," Harlan said. "Maybe you should consider a career in radio."

She laughed. "I don't think so. I've got enough on my plate."

"I was thinking maybe WFFM could do a remote show from your coffee shop every once in a while," Harlan said. "A kind of what's happening in the community thing. It'd let you promote that center of yours, and any other important things."

She thought about his offer. It touched her that he had listened to what was important to her, and was offering his help and support. And definitely something she could do. "Sounds like a good idea. Thank you."

He pulled off his hat and spun it between his fingers. "What you said back there, about dreams becoming reality, it made me think."

"About what?"

"About how you were right, Sophie."

An unbidden smile filled her face. "That's twice in one week you've said that, Mr. Jones."

"I'm really going to have to do something about you calling me by my last name."

How she wanted to fall back into the tease in his eyes, the grin on his face, the low, sexy notes in his voice. But the part of her that had been burned before danced away from the possibility. "I...I can't."

She spun toward the gazebo where dozens of couples were circling the floor in each other's arms. Harlan came up behind her. That man was determined and stubborn. She turned around. "Harlan, please don't—"

He put a finger over her lips, cutting her off. Sophie caught the scent of his cologne, fresh, clean and crisp, and the slightly salty taste of his skin before his hand dropped away. "It's not too late, Sophie. It's never too late to say you love someone."

"You...what?"

"You were right when you said I was afraid. All my life, I've been afraid of repeating my father's mistakes. I spent my life trying to earn the money he never did, and that made me as shy as a colt at a gunfight."

"That's why you've been reluctant to quit your job and go into furniture making full-time."

He nodded. "I didn't realize that by not going after what I really wanted, I didn't just hurt myself. I hurt the woman I love."

He'd said it twice. She still couldn't believe it. "You... you love me?"

"I do indeed, darlin'." He smiled, then took her hand, and led her up into the gazebo. He cradled one of her hands in his, placed the other against her back. "And if I'm going to say I love you, Sophie Watson, I'm damned well going to do it with you in my arms."

The band kept playing a sweet, slow song, and Harlan had begun to move in easy steps to the right, bringing her up against the heat of his body. The hard strength of him made her pulse skitter, her heart leap. "But…but we barely know each other."

"We've spent more hours together than most people do in a year. And besides, I don't need months and months to figure out what I want." His gaze met hers. "I want you."

His blue eyes held an intensity that told her every word was true. That this wasn't some kind of infatuation that would blow over with the first strong wind. That the man she had gotten to know in those quiet moments they'd had together was the real Harlan Jones.

She listened to her own heart, and heard a depth in there she'd never felt before. "I love you, too." Then she smiled, and added, "Harlan."

His answering grin nearly took her breath away. He leaned in and kissed her, a soft, sweet kiss that held promises of hundreds of wonderful tomorrows. "I'm glad to hear that, darlin'," he murmured against her mouth. "Damned glad."

She wrapped her arms around his neck and stared up into his eyes. She could look into that ocean for the rest of her life, and never tire of the view. "Me, too."

Harlan danced her around the gazebo and Sophie leaned against his chest, hearing the steady, dependable beat of his heart. "I do believe we have one more issue to settle."

"What's that?"

"A little matter of payment. I want two hundred dollars."

She leaned back and stared at him. "Two hundred dollars? For what?"

"My chairs. I'm going into the furniture business, and that means I gotta charge you for my work." His arms tightened around her and he pulled her into his chest so fast, she let out a little squeak. His gaze danced with laughter. "But considering you're my very first customer, I'll let you work off what you owe me with kisses."

"I can afford that." She rose on her toes and pressed a kiss to his lips. "There's my down payment."

"Mighty fine start," Harlan said. "I forgot to tell you, there's interest, too."

Sophie laughed. "Let me guess, biscotti?"

"You know it." He grinned, kissed her again, then swung her in a slow, easy circle as the band kept playing and the lights kept twinkling and the world around them fell in love.

Sophie leaned her head on the solid strength of Harlan Jones's chest. "Maybe I should start playing the lottery."

"Really? Why?"

"Because the first time I was lucky enough to win me a cowboy." She lifted her gaze to his, giving Harlan a flirty, teasing smile. "Who knows what I might get the next time?"

He brushed his mouth against hers and everything in Sophie's body stilled. "What more do you need, darlin'?"

"Nothing," Sophie murmured against his lips. "Nothing at all."

Coming Next Month

Available May 10, 2011

You can find more information on upcoming
Harlequin® titles, free excerpts and more at
www.HarlequinInsideRomance.com.

REQUEST YOUR FREE BOOKS!
2 FREE NOVELS PLUS 2 FREE GIFTS!

Harlequin *Romance*

From the Heart, For the Heart

YES! Please send me 2 FREE Harlequin® Romance novels and my 2 FREE gifts (gifts are worth about $10). After receiving them, if I don't wish to receive any more books, I can return the shipping statement marked "cancel." If I don't cancel, I will receive 6 brand-new novels every month and be billed just $3.84 per book in the U.S. or $4.24 per book in Canada. That's a savings of at least 15% off the cover price! It's quite a bargain! Shipping and handling is just 50¢ per book in the U.S. and 75¢ per book in Canada.* I understand that accepting the 2 free books and gifts places me under no obligation to buy anything. I can always return a shipment and cancel at any time. Even if I never buy another book, the two free books and gifts are mine to keep forever.

116/316 HDN FC6H

Name   (PLEASE PRINT)

Address   Apt. #

City   State/Prov.   Zip/Postal Code

Signature (if under 18, a parent or guardian must sign)

Mail to the **Reader Service:**
IN U.S.A.: P.O. Box 1867, Buffalo, NY 14240-1867
IN CANADA: P.O. Box 609, Fort Erie, Ontario L2A 5X3

Not valid for current subscribers to Harlequin Romance books.

**Are you a subscriber to Harlequin Romance books
and want to receive the larger-print edition?
Call 1-800-873-8635 or visit www.ReaderService.com.**

* Terms and prices subject to change without notice. Prices do not include applicable taxes. Sales tax applicable in N.Y. Canadian residents will be charged applicable taxes. Offer not valid in Quebec. This offer is limited to one order per household. All orders subject to credit approval. Credit or debit balances in a customer's account(s) may be offset by any other outstanding balance owed by or to the customer. Please allow 4 to 6 weeks for delivery. Offer available while quantities last.

Your Privacy—The Reader Service is committed to protecting your privacy. Our Privacy Policy is available online at www.ReaderService.com or upon request from the Reader Service.

We make a portion of our mailing list available to reputable third parties that offer products we believe may interest you. If you prefer that we not exchange your name with third parties, or if you wish to clarify or modify your communication preferences, please visit us at www.ReaderService.com/consumerschoice or write to us at Reader Service Preference Service, P.O. Box 9062, Buffalo, NY 14269. Include your complete name and address.

HRI1

*With an evil force hell-bent on destruction,
two enemies must unite to find a truth that turns
all-too-personal when passions collide.*

*Enjoy a sneak peek in Jenna Kernan's next installment
in her original* TRACKER *series, GHOST STALKER,
available in May, only from Harlequin Nocturne.*

"**W**ho are you?" he snarled.

Jessie lifted her chin. "Your better."

His smile was cold. "Such arrogance could only come from a Niyanoka."

She nodded. "Why are you here?"

"I don't know." He glanced about her room. "I asked the birds to take me to a healer."

"And they have done so. Is that *all* you asked?"

"No. To lead them away from my friends." His eyes fluttered and she saw them roll over white.

Jessie straightened, preparing to flee, but he roused himself and mastered the momentary weakness. His eyes snapped open, locking on her.

Her heart hammered as she inched back.

"Lead who away?" she whispered, suddenly afraid of the answer.

"The ghosts. Nagi sent them to attack me so I would bring them to her."

The wolf must be deranged because Nagi did not send ghosts to attack living creatures. He captured the evil ones after their death if they refused to walk the Way of Souls, forcing them to face judgment.

"Her? The healer you seek is also female?"

"Michaela. She's Niyanoka, like you. The last Seer of Souls and Nagi wants her dead."

Jessie fell back to her seat on the carpet as the possibility of this ricocheted in her brain. Could it be true?

"Why should I believe you?" But she knew why. His black aura, the part that said he had been touched by death. Only a ghost could do that. But it made no sense.

Why would Nagi hunt one of her people and why would a Skinwalker want to protect her? She had been trained from birth to hate the Skinwalkers, to consider them a threat.

His intent blue eyes pinned her. Jessie felt her mouth go dry as she considered the impossible. Could the trickster be speaking the truth? Great Mystery, what evil was this?

She stared in astonishment. There was only one way to find her answers. But she had never even met a Skinwalker before and so did not even know if they dreamed.

But if he dreamed, she would have her chance to learn the truth.

Look for GHOST STALKER by Jenna Kernan,
available May only from Harlequin Nocturne,
wherever books and ebooks are sold.

Fan favorite author
TINA LEONARD
is back with
an exciting new miniseries.

Six bachelor brothers are given a challenge—
get married, start a big family and whoever does
so first will inherit the famed Rancho Diablo.
Too bad none of these cowboys is marriage material!

Callahan Cowboys:
Catch one if you can!

The Cowboy's Triplets (May 2011)
The Cowboy's Bonus Baby (July 2011)
The Bull Rider's Twins (Sept 2011)
Bonus Callahan Christmas Novella! (Nov 2011)
His Valentine Triplets (Jan 2012)
Cowboy Sam's Quadruplets (March 2012)
A Callahan Wedding (May 2012)

Love Inspired.
HISTORICAL
INSPIRATIONAL HISTORICAL ROMANCE

Introducing a brand-new
heartwarming Amish miniseries,

AMISH BRIDES
of *Celery Fields*

Beginning in May with

Hannah's Journey

by ANNA SCHMIDT

Levi Harmon, a wealthy circus owner, never expected to find the embodiment of all he wanted in the soft-spoken, plainly dressed woman. And for the Amish widow Hannah Goodloe, to love an outsider was to be shunned. The simple pleasures of family, faith and a place to belong seemed an impossible dream. Unless Levi unlocked his past and opened his heart to God's plan.

Find out if love can conquer all
in HANNAH'S JOURNEY,
available May wherever books are sold.

INTRIGUE

WILL THE QUEST FOR THE KILLERS BE
TOO MUCH FOR THIS TOWN TO HANDLE?

FIND OUT IN THE NEWEST MINISERIES
BY *USA TODAY* BESTSELLING AUTHOR

B.J. DANIELS

WHITEHORSE MONTANA

Chisholm Cattle Company

Colton Chisholm has lived with the guilt
of not helping his high-school sweetheart
when she needed him most. Fourteen years
later, he's committed to finding out what
happened to her the night she disappeared.
The same night he stood her up.

BRANDED

May 2011

Five more titles to follow....

HI69543